I clung to the dollar bill folded into a cornucopia that held a snort of the stuff that looked like brown sugar. It burned in my hand. Sybil was watching me.

"Have a snort and snap out of it," she said.

"I'm off heroin," I said.

"You were never on," she answered. "Really."

While Sybil was watching me, I thought about Dr. Verdugo's warning. I heard his words clearly: "You had better get off the dope. If you don't, your baby will be born an addict. . . ." I got up and put the cornucopia on the shelf.

"I don't want it," I said. "I don't need it."

Kathleen,
please come home

Scott O'Dell

Published by
Dell Publishing Co., Inc.
1 Dag Hammarskjold Plaza
New York, New York 10017

Laurel-Leaf Library ® TM 766734, Dell Publishing Co., Inc.

ISBN: 0-440-94283-7

RL: 5.5

Reprinted by arrangement with Houghton Mifflin Company

Printed in the United States of America

First Laurel-Leaf printing—June 1980
Second Laurel-Leaf printing—July 1980

To Pixie Apt, unsung heroine,
and to all the girls who ran away.
To Kathleen and Joy and Tamara and
Daisy and Sybil and Linda. To all
the girls who came home and to
those who didn't.

Part I

These are the very first words in my new diary. I have never kept a diary before and I don't know whether I'll like it or not. Mother thinks I will. She says she's kept diaries since she was a girl and found them very helpful in getting her thoughts together.

Sometime I'd like to read them!

This is a special sort of diary.

It's one that Mother puts together herself. Every year, as long as I can remember, she's made up these diaries and sent them out to her friends. About 25 of them, at Christmastime. She gathers written messages from all over—poems, pieces of stories, famous sayings, and so forth—and puts them all down.

So there's a page with the day and the month, a space to keep a diary (if you fill up this space you can always turn the page over and write on the back) and one of these messages or poems or whatever. She puts these 365 pages together and has them Xeroxed and stapled.

But my diary is special. It has a blue leather binding and my name in gold letters on the cover. I'm going to take very good care of it. I really am. But I'll have to find a secret place to hide it from prying eyes.

January 2

Christmas vacation is over and it's back to the old grind.

I've a lot to show for my vacation, especially my good tan. All the girls will be jealous. Maybe I'll find myself a new boyfriend or two.

It was wonderful how Mother won that free trip to Hawaii, where she married Dad seventeen years ago.

She's always wanted to go back, especially now he's dead. And all she did was to write a poem for the Martin Motors contest. Four lines and she won a trip to Hawaii for two people, all expenses paid.

I think I'll become a poet, too. Wow!

January 3

All of the old faces are back—Melanie and Janet and Susan and Helen. Two new ones. Sybil Langley, who's from Seattle, and a boy named Jeffrey, who's from someplace like Chicago.

I liked Sybil right off. She has blond hair and gray eyes and is very sophisticated. Her father is Navy, and they've been transferred here to San Diego.

I like Jeffrey Thomas also. He's very handsome, though Sybil and Janet don't think so. Everyone to her tastes. His father is Navy too and has been transferred here. We have a lot to talk about. I think we're going to be good friends. I hope so!

January 7

It's been so hectic the last few days I haven't had the time or steam to put anything down in my diary. Mother asked me how I was coming with it, and I had to lie and say "Fine."

I must resolve not to miss a day from this time on.

I've seen a lot of Sybil. We're in the same classes and we eat lunch together in the cafeteria. She's my age but she's had many more experiences than I've had. At least she says so and I believe her. She thinks I've led a very sheltered life. I guess I have, come to think about it.

I've had a lot of studying to do, making up for the studying I didn't do just before Christmas when we heard about the free trip to Hawaii with all expenses paid and I couldn't think of anything except how I would lie on the beach at Waikiki and get a tan and go riding in an outrigger. Maybe catch a big wave.

January 10

I missed yesterday because I had a cold and nothing happened. And nothing has happened today, but I'll make a note of it just to keep up the sacred pact with my diary.

January 15

Wonderful! Wonderful! Sybil's father, who's a captain in the Navy, has gone off on sea duty. He'll be gone for six months. Meanwhile Sybil will have the full use of his brand-new four-wheel drive Blazer, which he used when he went hunting on the desert and down in Mexico.

Sybil took me riding in it last night for the first time. We went all around Shelter Island, then we stopped at McDonald's and had Cokes and hamburgers. We were home early, before nine o'clock, so Mother didn't say anything much.

I don't think she likes Sybil.

January 16

The message for today is from Katha Upanishad, 7th century B.C. "Know thyself as the Lord of the Chariot, the body as the chariot, the intellect as the charioteer, and the mind as the reins . . . He who understands the driver of the chariot and controls the reins of his mind reaches the end of the journey."

I wonder who Katha Upanishad is, was.

It doesn't matter. It's a good message for the New Year and I'll think about it every day, or try to. But first, I'll have to find out what "the end of the journey" means, particularly what it means for me.

January 20

Another gap in my diary, caused this time by the dentist, the orthedontist? (I am not sure of the spelling, but will look it up as soon as I get a dictionary. Perhaps on my birthday.)

He's taken out two impacted wisdom teeth. Instead of standing straight up like other teeth, they were lying down on their sides like little fish. Why are they called "wisdom teeth"? I guess they're

13

the only thing wise about me. At least two of my teachers seem to think so.

First it was Mr. Carrol. Now it's Miss Turner in English. I don't care about biology but I do care about English. Last year I got an A, now I am not doing so well, with a B on our first test.

Is it Jeffrey Thomas?

I don't think about him much but I still dream about him.

I'll have to pick up my grades before Mother hears about it. That's one thing she won't stand for—me getting less than an A in English. It doesn't look right, she says, for an English teacher to have a daughter who doesn't make top grades in English. Even though she teaches in junior high and I'm in high school.

It's super going everywhere with Sybil in her Blazer, so I had better shape up. Or get ready to stay home every night and study.

January 26

Another gap. This time no excuse. I guess I'd better plan to write in my diary only once every week, on Saturday maybe.

January 27

Oh Bliss! Oh Heavenly Bliss! My first date with Jeffrey. I can't wait. If I only had a new sweater.

January 28

We went to a heavenly new place down on Shelter Island. It's like a river boat, a paddle-wheeler, and everything. It's moored to a wharf. Inside there's a big room with a band at one end and a bar at the other end and a ferny fountain in the middle.

Jeffrey asked me what I wanted to drink. Since I'd never had a drink except a few glasses of sherry at home, I had to think. It was embarrassing because I wanted to act sophisticated.

Then I remembered a drink Sybil told me about. It's called a Spritzer, and it's made of white wine and seltzer water. "A keen drink," Sybil told me, "when you're on a first date and don't want to get bombed."

The music was way out and Jeffrey is a good dancer, but the trouble was, he kept talking about a girl he knew back where he came from. Her name is Kelly, which is an odd name for a girl. I guess it fits her though, taking into account what Jeffrey has told me.

First, it seems that he was engaged to this girl Kelly at one time and he gave her a ring to wear and she gave him a charm to wear.

The ring cost $25 but the charm cost $2000. I guess her family must have been rich.

Anyway, Kelly gave him this charm which was found down in Yucatan somewhere. It was dug up from a tomb belonging to a Mayan prince or a king, maybe.

The charm was solid gold, Jeffrey says, and about as big as a half dollar. It was in the shape of a woman without any clothes on, and made so you could pin it on your sweater or shirt or anything if you wanted to.

Anyway, she gave Jeffrey this pin, but he didn't like to wear it.

Although it was beautiful and very valuable, everyone who saw the charm made some kind of smart crack and he got embarrassed. So he put the charm away in a safe place and forgot it.

Then something very strange happened.

The two of them had had some sort of fight. Knowing Jeffrey, even a little, I would say that it wasn't his fault, and they parted forever and Jeffrey said that he'd never speak to her again so long as he lived. But before two weeks had gone by he caved in and phoned Kelly and wanted to know if he could see her and talk things over.

At first Kelly was cool to the idea, but she finally said yes and for him to walk over to the school and she would too, and they'd meet near the gym and talk.

Oh, another thing. Just as Jeffrey was hanging up, Kelly said, "Why don't you ever wear the charm I gave you? It's a very rare pre-Columbian artafact." So Jeffrey said, sure, he'd wear it and he did.

He pinned the artafact? (Whenever I come to a word I don't know how to spell, I am going to put a question mark after it and look it up when I get a dictionary, perhaps for Christmas) on his sweater.

This all happened early in the spring. But it happened near Chicago and not in California, so there were piles of snow under the trees and against the buildings everywhere. (Whew! This is getting to be a long story.) Anyway Jeffrey and Kelly met in front of the gym and stood and talked for a while.

Then Kelly said that she noticed that he was wearing the gold charm. The way she said it gave Jeffrey the suspicion that the only reason she had wanted to talk to him was to get the charm back.

Jeffrey unpinned the charm and handed it over to Kelly. "I guess you want it back, so here it is. Take it," he said.

Kelly was in a rage that he would think she was an Indian giver. She flung the charm away, out into a big mound of snow piled up against the gym. Just to show how much she was insulted.

Night had fallen, so finding a small object in a

snowbank was like finding a needle in a haystack, but Jeffrey ran over anyway and began to look around.

Kelly laughed at him and said she was going back home. Jeffrey gave up his hopeless search and followed her.

As the two ill-starred lovers (these are Jeffrey's words, not mine, thank heavens) stood on the porch of Kelly's house, he was putting his arms around her in a farewell embrace when his hand slipped under the lapel of her fur coat. Just by chance. He felt something hard. Suddenly he realized what it was. Kelly had not thrown the charm away. She had just gone through the motions, then pinned it under her lapel.

Jeffrey didn't let on to her that he knew what she had done. He just said good night and walked away. I wouldn't have walked away so meekly, you can bet. No, and I wouldn't still be talking about a girl who would do a trick like that. Dumb! Dumb! Dumb!

I've been thinking about it and come to the conclusion that Jeffrey has something missing upstairs.

Anyway, the evening wasn't as much fun as I thought it would be. As a matter of fact, it was a drag.

The message for today is a long quotation from George Bernard Shaw, which I can't make heads or tails of. I must learn not to use a preposition at the end of a sentence. It's one of the reasons,

Miss Turner says, for the poor grade I got on my last exam.

I'll watch it from now on and do the work I am capable of. Ha! Ha! I remember reading somewhere that Churchill got scolded once about this and said, "This is one correction up with which I will not put."

P.S. Jeffrey kissed me good night while we were standing out on the porch, but I'm pretty sure that he thought he was kissing Kelly. Come to think of it, it wasn't much of a kiss. Beforehand, he blew in my ear. My left ear. I wonder what this is supposed to do?

February 4

Another date with Jeffrey. He didn't mention Kelly once. He blew in both my ears this time. He must be leading up to something.

February 7

Big news! Next Saturday Sybil is taking us to the desert in the Blazer. Melanie, Helen, Susan, and me, five of us. We're going on Saturday and coming back Sunday. The only catch is Mother. I haven't asked her yet. I'll have to think about it hard and arrange everything so there'll be no foul-up. Melanie's parents are on the fence, but Helen and Susan both have permission. I'll suggest they call Mother. That will be the best way, I think.

February 9

Mother has given her permission for me to go. It wasn't easy, however. Mrs. Langley told Mother that Sybil knows her way around and has made the trip a dozen times. But Mother said no until Mrs. Langley said she would go along as a chaperone.

We'll have fun, anyway. I'd like to have a pair of hiking boots, but Mother says we can't afford them. I'm going to take my diary along and write in it by firelight.

February 12

I am writing by campfire. I got up at dawn and collected an armful of mesquite and put it on last night's coals. There was quite a blaze then and the smoke smelled good.

We're having fun because Mrs. Langley decided at the very last minute that she couldn't come. I can't wait until I put down all that happened yesterday. I am so excited I can hardly hold my pen.

But where to start?

I guess at noon, when we were eating the sandwiches we had put up. We were sitting there beside the Blazer, munching away and giggling about something that Sybil said—she is very funny and can mimic anyone. The sun was overhead and it was very hot. Off to the South toward the Mexican border, which was only five or ten miles away, there were some blue mountains. Between us and the mountains the air shimmered and rose from the sand dunes in curly waves.

Suddenly I saw something. I was the only one who did. A shape on the horizon, not more than half a mile away. I wasn't sure what it was so I pointed.

"What?" And everyone looked. "Where?"

"There," I shouted.

Nobody said anything. We all stared.

"It can't be a car, there's no road," Sybil said. "It must be an animal."

"Maybe a deer," Susan guessed.

I could have said, "It's a mountain lion," because there are lions out here sometimes, but I kept quiet.

The figure came on across the sand, moving slowly between the dunes. Then it disappeared.

Sybil said, "It must have seen us."

"Good," I said, still thinking that it might be a mountain lion.

We waited for a while. Then Sybil climbed on the hood of the car. She waved a scarf she was wearing. "It's a man," she said. "A man on a burro."

We waited some more.

"He's standing there," Sybil said. "But now he's coming along. It's an old man with a beard."

The man and the burro came from behind one of the sand dunes. They were close to us now.

The man was riding bareback and his legs were so long they touched the ground. The burro was white with alkali dust, and the man, who had a short beard, was white too.

I remembered a picture I'd seen of Don Quixote riding along in Spain. I realized that the two men looked alike, and it gave me a funny feeling.

The man came close and put his feet on the ground. Then he gave the burro a slap and the animal walked out from under him. It went a few steps, leaving the man standing there.

He was wearing a wide-brimmed sombrero, which he took off as he bowed to us. Then I saw that his hair was not white after all but black, and that he was not an old man but a very young man.

He spoke Spanish, which I understood after a moment. It had more harsh sounds than I had heard before. I understood him because I've spoken Spanish since I was eleven.

The young man said, "At first I thought you

were the Immigration. I am glad to see you are not. You have no men?"

"None," I answered. Then I thought better of it and said, "Our boyfriends have gone up the canyon."

"But they return?"

"They return."

"But they are not the Immigration?"

"No."

"My name is Ramón Sandoval," the young man said.

I introduced the girls one by one and he bowed to each of them. He brushed the dust off his shirt and slapped his sombrero against his leg and bowed again, low, as if we were queens.

"Do you have water for drinking?" he asked me.

"Water and Cokes. Which do you wish?"

"Cokes." While he was drinking the bottle I got for him he said, "You speak the language well."

"I have lived in Mexico."

"Where in Mexico?"

"In the port of Vera Cruz."

"I have heard the name. It is on the sea."

"Yes, on the Caribbean Sea. I lived there in Vera Cruz for a year."

He drank the Coke and I got him another out of the car and he drank that one, all the while walking around, stretching his legs.

His beard was short, more like a square goatee, if there is such a thing. He had a thin face with hollows in his cheeks. When he smiled, which he did most of the time he was standing there, he showed a lot of bright teeth.

He looked much older than me. He must have been eighteen anyway. He was wearing a shirt that had been white once, and what looked to be a cardboard collar, but wasn't. It was fastened with a silver button.

"Do you wish water for your burro?" I asked.

"He drank this morning. It is not good to spoil a burro," Ramón Sandoval said.

The burro nibbled at the license plate on the Blazer. The girls were getting impatient, especially Sybil, who said, "What are you yacking about?"

"Nothing much," I answered.

"I think we have a wetback on our hands. Find out."

"How?"

"Ask."

Ramón was watching the sandwich I had in my hand, so I offered him one half, which he took and ate in two bites. But when I offered him a sandwich out of the basket, he shook his head. I had a feeling, though, that he hadn't eaten for days.

Sybil gave me a look so I asked him. "Where do you come from?"

He waved his hand toward the blue mountains of Mexico. "*Por alla*," he said. He had a soft voice and stopped between words.

"How long are you on the road?"

He counted on his fingers, then held up all of them, once, twice, three times, and then added two more.

"Thirty-two days?"

He nodded.

"From where?"

"San Carlos. From a village near Rosalía."

"I have heard of Rosalía. It is far."

"Very far."

He walked over and took the halter from his burro's neck and a package wrapped in burlap. The burro had hoofs no larger than my fist and was so small it could walk under my outstretched arm.

"Your animal is not much for such a journey," I said.

"I have walked most of the way," Ramón answered.

He went over and sat down and leaned against the side of the Blazer. In a minute he was asleep.

(It looks like I'll fill up the whole diary with this one day.)

Later on

I am writing by the dim light from the fire. Everyone is sleeping, even the burro. There's a moon over in the west and a lot of stars. The evening was exciting. But that's not the right word for all the things that happened.

We had to wake Ramón up. He was all set to

sleep for days and days. We built up the fire with armloads of mesquite, then roasted wieners and toasted two dozen buns.

Ramón ate more than the rest of us put together. Afterward he brought the bundle he had taken off the burro. In it was a shiny guitar made of dark wood. He played a piece and sang in an out-of-tune voice. The piece is called "Espinita," which means "little thorn" in Spanish. It's a sad song but he seemed to enjoy it. I did, too.

While he was singing, Sybil took a joint out of her handbag. She had bought it from someone at school. I knew she smoked marijuana, because she had told me, but I was surprised when she brought it out in front of everyone.

She took a coal from the fire and lit the joint and held the smoke in her lungs and let it out slowly.

"From Culiacán," she announced, as if she were an expert, and held the cigarette out to Ramón, who shook his head.

"Smooth," Sybil said. "Try it."

I translated her words and Ramón said, "Many thanks, lady, but this one, Ramón Sandoval, he likes the world the way it is. It is a good world, no?"

Sybil passed the joint to me and I held it, watching the smoke curl up. It had a nice smell, like tea.

Sybil said, "Take a drag, dummy. It's no big problem."

"Come on," said Melanie.

"The joint's going out," Sybil said. "Fish or cut bait."

I glanced at Ramón. Fire shadows were on his face. He shook his head.

"Come on," Sybil said.

I put the cigarette between my lips. I wanted to show off.

"Breathe in."

I breathed in. The smoke stuck in my throat and I coughed and breathed in again. The smoke tasted the way it smelled, like tea. My mouth felt funny.

Melanie said, "How do you feel?"

"The way I did before."

"Nothing?"

"Nothing, except a funny taste."

"It's because you didn't inhale."

Melanie finished the cigarette.

I sat and waited, but nothing happened. Ramón began to play his guitar and I just relaxed and felt sophisticated.

February 13

I'm finally home, but I haven't finished with our trip.

Yesterday morning I was up early, before anyone. I went looking for wood for our breakfast fire.

We'd used all the wood that was handy, so I went down to a dry gully that looked as if it had a stream running through it sometimes.

The sun was just coming up over the mountains. They were dark blue against the sky, which was streaked with light. The morning was really beautiful. It seemed more beautiful to me than any morning in my whole life. Everything around me looked beautiful. The sky and the mountains and the way the sun touched the edges of the mesquite bushes. The way the morning breeze was fresh on my face. I felt alive all over.

I kept thinking of Ramón—how he'd looked when he was riding the burro, covered with alkali dust and swinging his legs, how I'd thought that he looked like Don Quixote, and how I'd felt when he played the guitar and sang.

Anyway, I had no trouble finding an armload of dry mesquite, and I was on my way back to camp, wondering why I didn't bring the burro and let him carry the wood, when I saw a snake lying coiled up right in front of me. I could have stepped on it, if something hadn't told me to look down.

Rattlesnakes are supposed to hibernate in February, but this one didn't get the word, I guess, because it was lying there with its forked tongue flicking in and out, looking at me with eyes that were like jet buttons.

I stepped back and almost dropped the wood.

The trail was narrow where I was walking, with high banks on both sides. I was standing there knowing that I couldn't go on when I remembered that someone, my father, had told me that rattlesnakes come in pairs. If you saw one, you'd better look around, because there would be its mate nearby.

I glanced in back of me. Then I glanced along the banks, which were even with my eyes. I was scared and really mad at myself because I was scared and then I was mad at the snake.

I dropped the armload of wood and picked up a piece of the mesquite and got ready to go after the snake. To kill it. I was a few feet away from it. Its head was raised up and was moving back and forth, getting ready to strike. The snake began to rattle—a sizzling sound.

In my excitement I must have let out a yell. I don't remember, but anyway Ramón heard something and the next thing I knew he was up on the bank telling me to stop. Then he jumped down and grabbed the stick from my hand.

"It is not good to kill things that mean no harm," he said. "The snake did not come upon you. You came upon it. It is not pursuing you. It is frightened also."

While he was saying all of this, he made a step with his hands and I put my foot in it and he swung me up. Then he tossed the firewood onto the bank and climbed up himself. I was shaking all over. I really was.

I thought Ramón Sandoval was crazy! But I felt bad about lying to him about our boyfriends, so I confessed that we didn't have any, really. He said he didn't think so. I don't know what he meant by that.

February 14

More about Sunday. It was quite a day!

After Ramón and I got back to camp and made a fire the trouble really started. (I must quit using "really" all the time. "It's a careless habit," Miss Turner says. I really must!)

Anyway, we ate breakfast and fooled around a while, taking our time packing.

Ramón put the halter on his burro. He expected to travel by himself, but I made the suggestion that he ride into San Diego with us.

"How?" asked Sybil. "We can't stuff his burro in the car."

"We can let it run along beside us," I suggested.

"At two miles an hour?" Sybil complained. "We wouldn't be home this week."

"We can leave it at a ranch," Susan said. "There's one two or three miles from here."

"Ramón's a wetback," I said. "The country around here is lousy with Immigration officers. He'll be picked up before he goes ten miles."

"So what?" Sybil said. "That's his problem."

"He's a nice guy," I answered.

Sybil gave me a wilting look. "So he's a nice guy.

What if he's carrying a pocketful of pot or maybe heroin? And we get stopped and all of us get busted and they confiscate the Blazer?"

"I'll ask him if he's got anything." So I did, and Ramón turned his pockets inside out and shook out his poncho.

Sybil went on grumbling, for which I didn't blame her because she was responsible for the car, but she gave in at last and we started off with the tailgate down and Ramón and me holding the halter and leading the burro.

We stopped at the first ranch, but there was no one home except a couple of barking dogs, and we started off for the next ranch, which was about two miles away.

It was noon now and the sun was hot, and everybody but me was bitching about dragging along at two miles an hour.

Two cops came up behind us. We saw them coming and Ramón gave me the halter and rolled back into the car and Melanie and Susan covered him with a blanket. The cops wanted to know what we were doing. Sybil said, "What's it look like?" But I, being more diplomatic, said that we were taking the burro up the road a mile or two.

The cops were very nice and fell in behind us and escorted us to the ranch. Sybil told the rancher that we'd found a burro wandering around on the desert and we would sell it for $25. He looked the animal over, saw that it had no brand, and gave us $15, which we gave to Ramón, who was glad to get it because he had only paid $3 for it.

Now the problem was, what were we going to do with Ramón the wetback?

We couldn't take him to the YMCA or leave him on the street corner somewhere to get picked up by the Immigration before the week was out. Finally Sybil said she could take him home and put him in a room up in the garage. For a night or two. And that is how the affair stands at this moment. Ramón is hiding in Sybil's garage.

I haven't told Mother about it yet.

February 17

A lot's happened since last Sunday. Ramón has a nice room. It's meant for a servant but Sybil's mother's maid left, so she's consented to let him have it for a while. There's a shower and a nice place to cook and a small view of the ocean. Ramón doesn't say much but he seems to like it. Maybe he's homesick. The problem now is to find him a job. He has the $15 from the sale of his burro. That's all!

February 19

The trouble with finding Ramón a job is that he doesn't speak English. Not a word. Maybe one or two, like "Hello–Goodbye," which won't do him much good.

And then there's the fact that he's an alien and hasn't any identification papers. Susan says that she thinks she can get him a set of fake ones with her father's help. But I don't see how that would do much good. If Immigration stops him and Ramón can't understand what they're talking about and can only say "Hello–Goodbye," they're going to know that he's a wetback.

February 25

Last night was my first date with Ramón, sort of. Sybil came along too, but it was really my date. The three of us went to an early show and saw a Woody Allen movie. Woody Allen said that swimming isn't a sport. It's something you do to keep from drowning. Afterward we went back to Sybil's house—her mother was away—and talked and played records.

We talked about the time on the desert when

33

we were sitting around the fire and Ramón wouldn't smoke the pot.

Sybil said to me, "Ask him if it's easy to buy pot where he comes from?"

I translated what she said, and Ramón replied, and I translated for Sybil. He threw up his hands in a big gesture and said, "It grows in the valleys and the hills and the mountains. It grows everywhere around San Carlos."

"If we went to San Carlos," Sybil said, "what would we pay for a pound of grass?"

"It is cheap. Ten dollars, maybe. My friends said to me, 'Ramón, if you go to the north, take marijuana. It is better than money."

Sybil was silent, figuring something in her head. Then she said, "A hundred pounds of grass at ten dollars a pound. If we went and bought a hundred and brought it back here, we'd be rich."

Ramón was surprised when I translated Sybil's idea. So was I. He said, "It is a long journey from San Carlos to this city. There are many *federales* between."

"But you're Mexican, Ramón. The Mexican cops won't hassle you. It's only gringos they hassle. I'd think that you'd like to make some money, being poor and everything."

Ramón finished his Coke, wiped his mouth, and put the bottle on the floor. "Your idea I do not like," he said. "I am here in Los Estados Unidos and I wish to remain here in Los Estados Unidos."

Sybil looked disappointed. "You came riding on

a burro from a village that's far away," she said. "You had a guitar. You had a wild look in your eye. I thought you must be someone who loves adventure. I guess I was wrong."

"Is it adventure," Ramón asked, "to be thrown in the *juzgado?* To be killed? Is this fun, señorita?"

"I see you're afraid," Sybil replied.

"*Si, yo tengo miedo,*" Ramón admitted. I didn't translate his words but just let them stand. I think Sybil understood that he was fearful.

She laughed and patted his shoulder as if everything she'd said was a big joke. We all laughed, but I wonder. (Sybil is very grown-up for her age. I wish I were as grown-up as she is. Of course, she's months older than I am.) I wonder if she isn't serious about going down to Baja and bringing back a stash of marijuana.

February 26

Sybil's mother has told Ramón to move. She's hired a new maid and needs the room.

February 27

We've found a place for Ramón.
Nearby, with Mrs. Bronson, a widow. He's go-

ing to do chores for her to pay for his rent. Susan said again that her father can get him a set of identification papers.

We're going to look for a real job right away.

It would be wonderful if Ramón could go to school.

But how can you go to school if you can't speak a word of English? It's hard enough if you do speak English!

Which reminds me that I must think about my classes. Miss Turner is beginning to give me the tiger-eye. Lucky that I have such a good memory. Miss Turner calls it phenomenal. "It's too bad," she says, "that you don't use it more."

Another thing. I must tell Mother about Ramón. I wish I had told her the day we came back from the desert. Now I have so much to tell her I don't know where to start. Maybe I'll wait and not say anything for a while.

Yesterday there was a poem. It gives me the shivers, the first part especially:

> In Xanadu did Kubla Khan
> A stately pleasure-dome decree:
> Where Alph, the sacred river, ran
> Through caverns measureless to man
> Down to a sunless sea . . .

I would like to be a poet and write poems like Samuel Taylor Coleridge. Perhaps that will be my life's ambition.

Jeffrey called and wanted me to go to a movie but I told him I had a headache.

February 28

Susan's come up with something that may be important. Her father has a contact with a Chicano, a man named Feliciano Diaz. Mr. Diaz is sort of a boss and he has 15 or 20 wetbacks working for him. He furnishes them with fake identification papers and finds them jobs and takes them to their jobs every morning in his Chevy truck and picks them up at night. For this service he asks 10 percent of their wages.

March 1

Mr. Diaz has taken Ramón on. Ramón will start work tomorrow. Hooray! I can tell Mother about him, now that he has a regular job.

March 2

I've told Mother. I picked the best time to tell her, which is after her second cup of coffee.

She was sitting in the living room, watching the weather report on TV. I asked her if I could get her another cup of coffee. She said, "No, thanks," still watching the TV. It wasn't a good beginning but anyway I started right in to tell her about how we picked up Ramón on the desert. And afterward. I expected her to say, "Why didn't you tell me about him before?" but she didn't. She just sat there staring at the TV.

"Today," she said, "is the fifth anniversary of your father's death. It was like this early in the morning when word came. It seems like yesterday."

"I know," I answered, though it didn't seem like yesterday to me. It was long ago, in another life I've lived. I wish Mother would find someone, some man she could like. I felt that it wasn't the time to talk about Ramón, so I got out the vacuum and cleaned my room and washed the dishes. Something I haven't done for a long time.

Jeffrey called and asked me to go to a track meet. I begged off.

March 9

Ramón got his first money. It came to $74.25 altogether, but Mr. Diaz took out 10 percent, then $50 for the fake identification papers, leaving less than $20, but Ramón is still pleased because in

Baja California he would have to work two weeks and more to make that much. He says he is rich. Next week he will really feel rich, unless Mr. Diaz takes out for something else.

March 10

They're giving a night class in beginning English at the high school twice a week. Ramón wants to go. He isn't afraid he'll be picked up as a wetback, but I am. He says that there are thousands of wetbacks in San Diego and he'll take his chances. I wish I weren't a worrier.

March 12

Ramón has enrolled in the English class. I went over with him and helped him register. The teacher is a Mexican-American, which is better, I guess, than if she were just an American speaking Spanish. But maybe not. I'm going to class with him until he gets used to things.

Mother doesn't like it very much, this two nights in the middle of the week. But I'm home by nine o'clock. She hasn't said anything right out, but I'm sure she doesn't like the idea of me going to class with Ramón. Or anywhere else for that matter.

If she says that I have to stop going out with him, what will I say to her?

March 16

Mr. Diaz has given Ramón the pay for his second week. This time Mr. Diaz has taken out $20 for another paper and $5 for gasoline. But Ramón is happy. He wants to send some of the money to his mother, who has to work to support the family because Ramón's father doesn't work much. I must find out how he can send the money without its being stolen along the way.

March 23

Ramón proudly showed me a handful of cash for his third week of work. This time Mr. Diaz has deducted $19 for something or other.

A few weeks ago, on March 1, there was a remark in my diary by Jonathan Swift which seems to apply to Mr. Diaz: "I never wonder to see men wicked, but I do wonder to see them not ashamed." But Ramón doesn't think that it's a good idea to say anything. Mr. Diaz might get mad and turn him over to Immigration.

March 25

Ramón is doing well at night-school. He's learned a lot of English words, but he has trouble putting them together.

Also trouble with words like "still," which mean two or three different things. I mean, it can mean "quiet" or "yet" or a thing to make alcohol.

Also he has trouble with his pronunciation. And he goes up the scale when he should go down.

But he's learning. I help him by speaking English a lot.

March 27

Ramón has sent the first money to his mother. I helped him make out the money order. I wonder if the money will ever get there. And if it does, will his mother use it sensibly. I *am* getting to be a real worrier. Like Mother.

March 30

Nothing much on March 28 and 29, and ditto for today.

April 1

April Fool's Day and I was the one to get fooled. Trusting me!

Home Ec is the first thing in the morning. I was late getting up so I didn't have any breakfast and by the time I got to class I was really hungry. Mrs. Stanley gave us a choice of making cookies or brownies. I chose the brownies and so did Sybil. We've never made them before and it was fun. We made a lot—three dozen—and I planned to give Ramón some.

The first batch came out a little crisp but tasty. Sybil didn't eat any of hers but I was ravenous and ate two of mine quick. They hadn't much more than settled in my stomach when my head began to feel funny, as if it belonged to somebody else.

It wasn't a bad feeling, just strange.

Sybil had a mysterious smile. I smiled too. We stood there smiling at each other.

The school band was practicing in the gym. It usually makes an awful racket, but this morning the music sounded super. They were playing the USC marching song. Each note hung there sharp and bright, with sunny edges around it.

It seemed as if we were standing there for a long time, smiling at each other. But it was only a moment or two because I had the timer on the second batch of brownies and it started to ring.

I had a strong desire to open my mouth and laugh. Sybil shook her head. She pointed at the teacher and whispered, "April Fool."

But I didn't catch on until class was over and we were walking down the hall and Sybil said, "If you had eaten another you'd be walking on the ceiling."

I was so dumb that I still didn't know what had happened to me until Sybil explained that she'd put hash in the brownie batter. I didn't know she was into hash, too.

When I got home in the afternoon Mother was there. I usually kiss her but today I was afraid that she'd smell the stuff on my breath or on my clothes somehow, not knowing anything about it.

I have a strange feeling, even now, hours later as I sit here writing before I go to bed. It's not that I feel the way I did, even a little bit, but just thinking. I don't know whether I like hash or not. I wonder if Sybil uses it all the time or just now and then for kicks. I'll ask her tomorrow.

April 2

I saw Sybil today but didn't have a chance to talk to her because she was with some girls. I've seen them before around school, but I don't know their names.

April 3

Jeffrey called and wanted me to go out riding this afternoon, down to the desert where the wild-flowers are in bloom. I like wildflowers but not Jeffrey, so I said that I was busy.

I wish it were Ramón who'd called. I haven't seen him for three days. After his garden work for Mr. Diaz he's been clerking in Old Town, selling curios and stuff to tourists. He's saving his money now to get some wheels. Maybe he'll get a car so we can go down to Borrego before the flowers stop blooming.

Ramón's worth ten of Jeffrey. Of anyone I've ever known.

April 5

Talked to Sybil this morning in Home Ec. She was still laughing about me and the brownies. Little Linda Sanders knows about it. She saw me eat the brownies and then act funny. When I see her now she looks at me in a curious way, as if I have two heads.

April 8

Ramón has bought a '68 Ford on time, through Mr. Diaz, who charged him $25 for the service of guaranteeing his credit. Now he has to get a driver's license. He can drive a car but I'll have to go along to interpret. But what if he gets picked up by Immigration???

April 12

Ramón passed his driver's test yesterday and has a temporary license. We are going down to Borrego next Sunday to see the wildflowers. The papers say they are more wonderful this year than any year for a long time.

April 13

This afternoon I talked to Sybil. She was coming out of the auditorium after assembly. We both had ten minutes before our next classes so we sat down on the steps, off by ourselves. Sybil had a new hairdo. She had long beautiful hair that came

45

down almost to her waist. Now it's piled up on her head.

"Do you like it?" she asked.

"Yes," I said, trying hard to be enthusiastic. "It makes you look older." Sybil smiled her slow (Mona Lisa?) smile, so I knew I'd pleased her. "A lot older. Maybe a year older."

"Did you have any report from the brownies?" she asked me.

"Nothing much, except a little headache."

"That always happens at first. But you get over it. I did the second or third time. After that it's nothing but fun."

"It's the first time the band ever sounded good," I said.

We both laughed.

"I'm afraid Mother will find out," I said. "Linda Sanders saw me acting funny. She knows Mother and she might just tell her."

"That wouldn't be the end of the world. My mother found out a year ago that I was using. She's a screamer and every once in a while she screams. So what? I tell her that it's no worse than what she does—drinking two double martinis before dinner and then slopping up a half-dozen drinks afterward."

"My mother's not a drinker," I said. "So that argument won't work with her."

"Don't argue. Play it cool. If she finds out, just say you've quit."

I didn't realize until afterward that I must have

given Sybil the idea that I intend to go on eating brownies, which I really, most certainly, do not intend to do. Ever.

April 14

I am still thinking about the brownies and what Sybil said.

Today I bought a new pair of slacks, a heavenly shade of blue. I'll wear them to the desert. I hope Ramón doesn't find that he has to work at the last minute.

April 16

I can't wait until Sunday!

April 18

Ramón and I got an early start for the desert. There was fog along the coast and in the mountains but it was clear and sunny at Borrego.

The desert was a carpet of wildflowers, every kind possible and every color of the rainbow, as far as you could see in all directions. The yellow lilies I liked best. You can't pick them, though, because it's against the law, and they wilt anyhow before you can get them home.

It was a wonderful day. The most wonderful day of my life.

Ramón looked so handsome in the new leather jacket he'd bought.

It was hot but he wore it anyhow, until we found a place under a big saguaro cactus tree and sat down to eat our lunch, which I had gotten up at six to prepare. Ramón likes peanut butter (ick!), so I made him four sandwiches of it, with thick slices of bread and hunks of lettuce and gobs of jelly. He drank three Cokes (he can never get enough, it seems) and finished the sandwiches. I didn't eat much. I was too excited.

Ramón took a short siesta, but I stayed awake, looking at the sky and dreaming about things.

When he woke up, Ramón was quiet for a while. Then he said, speaking slowly in English, "You know what, Kathleen?"

"No," I said, "what?"

"Well . . ."

I waited, sort of afraid because he was serious, which he isn't most of the time.

"If we were down there in San Carlos," he said in Spanish, "I would speak different. It would take me a long time to say what I say now. But here in this country everything is very quick."

He used the English word for "quick" and asked me how it sounded.

"Good," I said, "like an Americano." But I was still afraid because he was so serious.

"In San Carlos I would speak to your parents first." He paused. "But here I speak to you." He took my hand in his. Carefully, as if it were something very precious that might drop and break. "I want you to be my bride," he said. "Mrs. Ramón Sandoval. How does that sound? Huh?"

My good memory has failed me for some reason and I don't remember what I said or what I did. I might have just sat there. Stunned, as I mostly am now. Too stunned to write anything clearly.

I remember that Ramón was still holding my hand and asking me again, and I said that I was in love with him. Since the day I saw him riding out of the desert. Since that time and now. Now at this moment, especially now, and forever.

Then Ramón kissed my forehead and my cheeks and my throat. They were all soft kisses, not the kisses I dreamed about sometimes, the kind that would make my toes curl up, but gentle and sort of friendly.

The sun went down and there was a slender little moon hanging upside down above the mesa. Ramón pointed it out to me as if he had just invented it. We sat there among the flowers and the tall saguaros for a long time. Not saying anything. Just sitting there like two happy kids drifting along on a raft. But I guess that both of us were thinking all the time about making love because soon, when dusk came and it grew dark, we fell into each other's arms, suddenly and fiercely.

April 19

I intended to tell Mother about Ramón when I got home from school, but she'd had a bad day and I thought it would be the wrong time to say anything.

The golden desert lilies that Ramón picked for me have faded, but I'll keep them alive in my diary. For April 17 there was a poem I liked. It's by William Blake. The first part is:

Tyger! Tyger! burning bright
In the forests of the night,
What immortal hand or eye
Could frame thy fearful symmetry?

I've started a poem in my head. I thought about it in math this morning. Remembering the lilies Ramón picked for me, remembering everything. It starts like this:

Golden lilies shining bright
In the desert of delight.

I'll work on it tomorrow when I'm not thinking

about what I'll say to Mother, which I must do. I must!

April 20

I put off telling Mother. She's gotten over her headache, so tomorrow will be a good time. As good as any time will ever be!

April 21

I got up my nerve after supper. Mother was grading some exam papers. My heart was in my throat. I've read those words somewhere in a story but I never believed them. Now I do.

I tried to be cool, as if it wouldn't be the end of the world if she said no. Which it would be. She knows that I had gone down to the desert with Ramón to see the wildflowers, but she didn't know that we went alone, just the two of us.

"Mother," I said, "I have some news."

She didn't look up.

"It's about Ramón."

She went on writing comments in the corners of the paper she was reading.

"He wants me to be his wife," I said.

It was a moment before Mother looked up.

"You should feel honored," she said, giving my frayed jeans and torn plaid shirt a critical glance. She'd been bugging me about the way I dressed. "Did he ask you to be his wife when you were looking as you do now?"

She was trying to be cool about things, so I came back cool to her, as much as I could under the circumstances. "His eyesight isn't very good," I said.

"Did you set a date?"

I could tell that she was going to try to make me feel ridiculous.

"No, I wanted to talk to you first."

She looked at me now in a different way. For the first time she saw that I was really serious. She laid the exam papers on the table and put the cap on her pen. A ship was hooting in the harbor. I waited until it stopped.

"Ramón is in love with me and I am in love with him," I said. "We want to get married."

Mother had a very patient look, the kind you need, I guess, if you have to get along with a hundred dizzy kids every day. But she still couldn't believe her ears.

"Do you have to get married just because you're in love?" she asked.

"No, I guess not. But I want to."

"You're not eighteen yet. You're not even sixteen. You can't get married when you're just a child. How old is Ramón?"

"Seventeen, I think."

Mother was silent. She looked at the floor. Then she looked at me suspiciously. "There's no reason why you have to get married, is there?"

"No, Mother."

She seemed relieved. At least she didn't ask any more questions on that subject.

"Ramón has a job," I said. "He can support me."

"That's encouraging."

"We'd like to get married in September."

"So you won't have to go to school next semester?"

"No, it's because . . . By then we'll have enough money saved up to take a honeymoon trip and get an apartment and furniture."

"You'll be sixteen by September."

"Sixteen going on seventeen."

"That's young to get married and have children . . ."

"I'm not going to have any for a while."

"You hope not. Of course, if you have children at your age it would be fun to grow up with them. You'll be a family of children growing up together. And I'll babysit for all of you."

She picked up her exam papers and shuffled them about and put them down again.

"Ramón's awfully young, Kathleen. You've known him only for a few weeks."

"For more than two months, Mother. Since February the eleventh. Just after twelve o'clock, noon."

"For a very short time."

I waited. My heart was bobbing around in my throat again. Mother picked up the exam papers.

"I will think about it," she said. "I want you to be happy."

"Girls my age and boys Ramón's age get married in Africa and India and South America. All the time. Every day."

"We are not living in Africa, India, or South America," Mother said. "I want to be certain before I consent. Remember that you are all I have."

I wanted to say that she had a lot more to live for than just me, that she had her own life, her school and work. But I didn't. In a quick thought I looked ahead. I saw a life for myself where I was all the life my Mother had.

"Say, yes, please," I said.

"I will think about it, Kathleen."

And that's where I stand on the twenty-first day of April in the Year of Our Lord, 1977.

April 22

Ramón and I went over to Point Loma tonight. (I told Mother that I was off to an interclass game.) The sun was going down behind the islands. I told Ramón about my talk with Mother and that I thought she would give us her consent.

Ramón looked very handsome in his new jacket

and his shiny black boots. I love the way his eyes look straight at you, not off somewhere.

"What if your mother does not give permission?" he asked me.

"I haven't thought."

"I have thought. I am thinking about it now. I am thinking hard."

"What if she says no?"

"If that happens we leave this place. We marry in the cathedral of Tijuana and go to San Carlos. It is a long way to San Carlos but it is a beautiful way. There are many white beaches. There are bays with blue water in them. There are mountains . . ."

We sat on the cliff and watched the sun go down and the big light come on in the lighthouse. We made heavenly love. It's a big wonder that the rocks didn't melt away.

But now I am scared. What if Mother says no?

April 23

Last night I woke up excited and after a while, thinking of Ramón, I remembered a poem by John Keats that was in my diary on March 10. The first lines I said to myself over and over.

I arise from dreams of thee
In the first sweet sleep of night,

When the winds are breathing low,
And the stars are shining bright.

I like John Keats. I wonder who, whom he was
in love with?

April 24

We were going to the beach today but Ramón
had to work at the shop. At least he made $11.

April 26

Sybil has started a club. Her mother corres-
ponds with a guru in India somewhere and Sybil
is using one of the letters he wrote to her. We're
to have a priestess, who will be Sybil, and also two
acolytes and we'll meet every tenth day, no matter what.

One of the things each member must do is cut
her fingernails and save the parings. Each nail must
be cut carefully and put in a little box and kept
safe somewhere, I don't know why yet. The club
is to be very secret. I'm not supposed to tell anyone, but I *am* going to tell Ramón.

The idea of the club, which is called Lotus, is
the development of the soul. I'm not too excited

about the idea, but Sybil is and so are my friends. I'll go along with it for a while, until September, anyway. I really can't think of anything except Ramón Sandoval. Kathleen Sandoval!

April 28

It's vacation time, and Mother and I went out to Sea World this afternoon to watch the dolphins perform. It's truly remarkable how they can train these wonderful creatures. My biology teacher said once that you can train humans the same way. Rewards and punishment—conditioning, he called it. I wonder if Mother is trying to condition me about Ramón. She didn't mention him once, the whole time, but she was thinking. I could tell. She's usually quiet around me, but today she kept jabbering about this and that. I guess she was trying to make up for all the times when she's sat and said nothing. Just silent with her own thoughts.

I feel sorry for her somehow. If I leave, she'll be alone. Maybe that would be better. Then she might find someone. . . . But I can't think of everything. I've got to lead my own life!

May 3

Vacation is over and we've had the first formal meeting of Lotus. It's so secret that I was forbidden even to write about what went on. It will be very mysterious. School? I will study like mad, especially math that I got a B in (in which I got a B?).

May 4

Today I talked to Mrs. Constable at Shelter Island. She has a women's shop called Turf and Surf, and she said that she'll hire me half-time when school is over. I'll make $2.75 an hour and save every cent of it. Horray!

May 6

Ramón and I took a walk along the beach at Del Mar after he was through work. The tide was out and we were walking along in our bare feet when suddenly he stopped and took out a little velvet box. In it was a ring. A ring with a single beautiful pearl. He put the ring on my finger and now we are officially engaged! I cried, I was so happy. I feel like crying now. I *am* crying.

May 9

Mother's noticed my ring. She must have, but she hasn't said anything. It's beautiful. It looks like a misty morning when the sun is coming up.

May 13

Lotus has voted to stage a party next Friday night. Each member can bring a boyfriend. I will bring my fiancé. Wow! That will give them something to think about.

May 21

The Lotus party was a disaster. I'm lucky to be alive.

All the girls had dates except Melanie, whose boyfriend checked out for some reason. Maybe he knew something beforehand.

Anyway, Sybil's mother went to play bridge

and it was the new maid's night off. We had the run of the house. Sybil pulled down the shades and turned off the lights, all except a blue-colored one in the library. Blue is our official color.

There were eleven of us altogether. Things started out slow, about as exciting as Evel Knievel jumping over cars on his motorcycle, but they began to pick up as soon as Sybil passed the Cokes.

They came in teacups—very delicate, white Chinese cups—on a big brass tray. Sybil hadn't said anything, but I guessed this was all part of the Lotus ceremony.

I don't like Cokes, so I was holding mine, turning it around and watching the blue light shining through the edge of the cup, thinking that after I was married maybe sometime I might be able to afford a set of lovely cups like it.

Ramón drinks a lot of Cokes—they have them way off in the mountains where he lived in San Carlos—but he didn't drink his either. He took a sip and then just sat there looking at it.

He said to me in Spanish, "There's something no good in the Coke. What I taste is no good. It is bad."

Ramón took the Coke away from me. There was a pot behind us with flowers in it, and after a while, when no one was looking, he dumped it into the pot. He dumped his in, too. We sat there until someone put a handful of records on and then we put our cups down and began to dance.

Sybil didn't pass out any more of the Cokes,

but she poured some in a punch bowl and invited everyone to partake. Ramón and I kept dancing and I sort of lost track of what was going on. Except that with all the talk and the shouting and the loud music, the room began to jump.

Everyone was helping himself, herself to the punch but Susan and her date and the two of us. But when Ramón went off looking for the bathroom, Sybil came up and asked me why I wasn't drinking. Before I could answer she ladled out a drink and put it in my hand.

"Don't be a square," she said and walked away.

Suddenly I remembered all the fun I'd had with the brownies, how everything seemed so funny and the awful band had sounded like a symphony. It was a very strong memory, stronger than any memory I had ever had.

I glanced around to make sure that Ramón hadn't come back. When I didn't see him, I swallowed the punch. I swallowed it quickly, wiped my mouth, walked over to the door, and waited for Ramón to come back.

I remember standing in the doorway. That is clear in my mind. Ramón came back and I remember that too.

We went and sat down on a fluffy cushion, off in a corner. I sort of remember that I saw Melanie dancing in the middle of the room. She was dancing by herself, I think. And she had taken off her sweater and was dancing with her big breasts bobbing up and down.

61

After that it's all mixed up, like in a long, slow dream.

I had a book of poems in my hand and I was reading to Ramón. Each word was in a little square. Each square was a different color—pink and blue and red and purple and other colors, too. The page looked beautiful, every word a lovely hue and every line blending together.

As I spoke the poem, the words glided out of my throat and hung in the air. They no longer were little squares but hovering butterflies that looked like jewels. Oh, so sweet and beautiful!

As I finished the poem, Ramón seemed to move away from me, and Melanie no longer was dancing alone, but with many young girls. I began to dance with them, holding hands around a Maypole that looked like a stick of peppermint candy, only bigger.

Music came from far off. It was the music of the stars rubbing together, touching, lingering, kissing—millions of stars, and I was a star, too, the very center of all the worlds God had ever created.

It was a heavenly moment that seemed to last a million, million years.

Then burning crystals of light in the shape of a chariot bore me away and I crossed a sea that burned with fire to a green jungle that was cool and sparkled with dew that was really diamonds and the fruit on the trees was real emeralds and rubies.

Then I wove a basket out of palm fronds and

packed it full of precious sparkling gems. I was richer than anyone in the world, than anyone who ever lived, than Croesus.

I must have hidden the basket because next I was on a roller coaster, like the one in Long Beach that I rode on once, only this time it had a loop-the-loop and we came to the loop and I hung there for a long time upside down, like the fruit on a tree. But I wasn't scared. Then an angel's hand plucked me from the tree and I floated earthward like a dandelion puff in a soft, soft breeze full of friendly voices and the odors of all the perfumes in the world.

Now, many hours later, I'm home, and orange-colored crabs with steel-tipped claws are crawling up and down my back.

Mother put me to bed, after giving me two glasses of warm milk, but after she went to sleep I got up to write in my diary. It is now three in the morning.

Ramón must have brought me home for I seem to remember Mother shouting at him on the front porch. I must tell her that it wasn't his fault. I must tell her everything. But what can I tell Ramón?

Oh, God, please help me.

I am going to sleep now. I'll try very hard. Things are crawling around in my head, though. They tread very carefully, but they have heavy feet and they hurt. I hope I feel better tomorrow.

What can I say to Ramón?
I can't write any more now.

May 22

I felt better today. Shaky but better. Ramón
doesn't like to phone, but he could have come to
see me. I've made a resolve: never, never, so long
as I live, will I ever under any circumstances drink
anything or eat anything with pot or hash in it.

One fortunate thing. Mother hasn't spoken about
last night.

May 23

I learned from Sybil today that it wasn't hash
she slipped in the punch. It was PCP.

Ramón didn't come by. Please, God, make him
come by. If he doesn't, I'll go to his house and sit
on the doorstep until he talks to me, if I have to
sit there until I am an old, old woman.

Mother still hasn't bawled me out.

May 25

Ramón got off from work early and we went out to Point Loma and walked around through the cemetery when I got home from school. He was very understanding about the other night. But he made me promise that I would never use pot or hash or LSD or PCP or anything. I promised him solemnly, holding a hand across my heart. He told me some stories that scared me out of my wits. I am scared out of them good. PCP or LSD he didn't know about, but he said that all of it was bad, and he made me swear again that I would never use dope. Ever again.

I'm so lucky to have someone like Ramón who knows about these things.

We made love in the cemetery, under a cypress tree. Beautiful! My head is still going round.

May 26

Mother has called Sybil's mother and told her what happened at the Lotus party. Now Sybil can't use the Chevy Blazer for a whole month. But Mother hasn't said anything more to me. She doesn't need to! We've decided to postpone the next meeting of Lotus.

May 28

I got an A on my math paper, which shows what I can do when I put my mind to it. I'm lucky to have a mind left! Sybil got a D, and her mother is screaming.

May 31

Five more days of school. Then morning classes at summer school, which Mother insists that I take. And I'll start in the afternoons at Turf and Surf. Save my money. Ramón and I will both be saving. I'll begin a savings account somewhere so I'll draw interest. By September we'll have a nice nest egg. Ramón is afraid to put his money in the bank. I don't know where he puts it. Under the mattress? I hope not.

June 4

School is over, hooray!

Ramón has had to work late every night this week. This is the beginning of the tourist season and the sightseers are flocking into Old Town, which is not so much an old town as a new town made to look old.

June 6

It's Sunday and Ramón is working at the tourist trap. I miss him, but another day, another dollar, as the saying goes. He is not sending as much to his mother now. He thinks that his father is trying to get money from her for some scheme or other.

June 8

Terrible! Mr. Diaz called this morning early and asked me if I knew why Ramón hadn't come to work yesterday. I said I didn't know and called his landlady, who was making such a commotion

I couldn't understand her. So I went over to the house in a hurry. She met me at the door and told me that two officers had come late yesterday afternoon and arrested Ramón for being an alien with faked identification and work papers. They gave him half an hour to pack up and make one phone call. The call was to me, but I was at Turf and Surf working. The landlady said that he asked her to tell me he would write as soon as he could.

When will that be? He can't write very well but I suppose he can get someone to write for him.

I am sick. I wish I could talk to Mother about it, but if I do she'll make me feel worse. She'd probably say, "What do you expect, if you get engaged to an alien who's running around with false papers?"

June 9

I didn't go to work today. I went to the Immigration Office at eight o'clock but it wasn't open.

It opened at 9:30 and I talked to a girl at the desk, who looked at some papers and found Ramón Sandoval on a list of aliens who had been sent off on a bus that morning at eight o'clock. Destination Hermosillo, Sonora.

I asked her why Ramón was sent to Sonora when his home was in Baja California. "That's where the bus is going," she said. "To Hermosillo."

Then I went to look for Mr. Diaz, but I couldn't find him.

June 10

I found Mr. Diaz this morning. He was doing some work at the school. I didn't have to tell him that I was frantic. That I am out of my mind.

"Ramón was the best worker we had," he said.

He chewed one end of his mustache for a while. "Perhaps we can get him back," he said. "I get them back sometimes. But it takes a little money. Not much, but a hundred dollars maybe."

I told Mr. Diaz that I would find the money. He said there was no hurry, but I went to Mrs. Constable right away and told her everything and she gave me two weeks' wages in advance.

I don't want to go to summer school, but Mother still insists. And Mother always knows best. Maybe.

June 11

I handed $100 over to Mr. Diaz this noon.

He said that he had found out that Ramón was in San Luis, which I have learned is a border town in Mexico, north of Hermosillo. He will send the money to San Luis by wire, to his friend there, who will get things started so Ramón can return to the U.S.A. But his friend will need $50 more some time soon. Like next Monday.

Besides being frantic, I am puzzled. I am beginning to wonder if Mr. Diaz kept the $100 and will keep the $50 next Monday. I wonder if he is the one who turned Ramón's name over to the Immigration. Horrible thought! If I could only talk to someone.

June 12

I scraped up $22 today. Summer school is a drag.

June 13

I told Sybil about Ramón and Mr. Diaz and the money. She said it is a big ripoff. "Let's go down and find Ramón," she said.

"You don't have the keys to the Chevy."

"I know where they are," Sybil said.

This whole thing worries me sick. I'm scared.

June 14

I got $8 more from Mother and $5 that Melanie owed me and took them to Mr. Diaz. That made $35. Mr. Diaz said that he would trust me for the rest and that he might need about $50 more, depending on certain matters in San Luis that he couldn't tell about now. I asked him if Ramón was safe. He said, "Sure, sure. My friend in San Luis will see that the health of Ramón Sandoval remains good."

June 15

No word from Ramón. Nor from Mr. Diaz. I am slowly going crazy. And not so slowly, either! Another week and I'll *be* crazy. I can't keep my mind on school.

June 16

Mr. Diaz dropped in at suppertime.
Wonderful news! Ramón is safe!
Mr. Diaz's friend in San Luis is sending him by

truck with nine others to San Diego. Ramón and the nine men will go first to a place east of Tijuana and wait there south of the border until it is safe to cross over into the U.S.

Ramón will be home inside of seven days, Mr. Diaz predicts.

As he was leaving, Mr. Diaz said that there were three parties in it who must be paid, so he must have another $100.

"You do not need to give me the money at this time," he said. I guess he saw the surprise on Mother's face. "Later will be good."

Mother looked at me. She was still surprised. "How much did you give Diaz?"

I counted up. "One hundred and thirty-five dollars."

Before Mother could speak, Mr. Diaz bowed and was gone. She didn't say anything for a long time. I could hear Mr. Diaz shifting gears as he drove away. He seemed to be in a great hurry. I guess it's not so much what he does as what his friend in San Luis does.

Mother said, "You have to expect this sort of thing as long as you think of marrying an alien."

"I'm not just thinking about it, Mother. I am going to marry Ramón."

She sipped her coffee. "Where do you plan to live when you get married?"

"I haven't thought much about that," I answered.

"It's not a bad idea to give it some thought.

Ramón may want to live in the village, whatever its name, the village he came from. Have you ever lived in a Mexican village?"

"I lived in Vera Cruz."

"Vera Cruz is not a village, as you well know. I mean in a village where the chickens and goats run around through the house, and when you go to the bathroom you use a hole outside somewhere."

I didn't answer, so that was about all that was said on the subject. Luckily Mother had to hurry off to a school meeting.

In seven days, or possibly before, Ramón will be home. I hardly believe it!

June 17

Six days more!

June 18

Five days!

73

June 19

Mr. Diaz came by this afternoon on his way to church. He said he had news from his friend that the truck was waiting at a place near Tecate, right on the border. And that Ramón should cross in three or four days.

He didn't ask for money.

June 20

This morning Mother was eating breakfast and looking at the paper. She made a funny noise and read aloud to me about two Mexican Immigration officers who had been shot at by some American Immigration officers.

It was sort of complicated, but from what I could figure out the Mexicans planned to cross the border and raid a camp where a bunch of wetbacks were waiting for a truck. The Americans got wind of the scheme somehow—it seems that the Mexicans planned to shake down the wetbacks—then they lay in wait and shot at the Mexicans with high-powered rifles.

Mr. Diaz didn't come by today, so everything

must be all right. I am not going to worry. At least I'll try not to.

June 21

No news from Mr. Diaz.

June 22

Mr. Diaz's truck pulled up this morning while we were still in bed.

I put on my robe and ran to the door. Mr. Diaz got out and came up the walk with his hat off. He looked pale, and before he spoke I knew something terrible had happened. I don't remember much of what he said.

Anyway, there had been another ambush on the border at Tecate. American officers had shot at the Mexican officers. One of the Mexicans was killed and two of the wetbacks were wounded. One of the wounded was Ramón. I asked him where Ramón was and he said that he was in Tecate. In a hospital there.

The rest of the day. . . . But why try to put it down in words? Why make it happen twice?

I called Mrs. Constable and told her I would not come to work.

Mother said she would take me to Tecate, but Mr. Diaz said it was better for him to take us.

He went off to gather up his workers.

He was gone until noon. When he returned, we were waiting.

He said he had very bad news for us. He spoke the truth.

Ramón is dead! He died in the hospital!

June 24

Mr. Diaz thinks that he can arrange for me to go to the funeral.

June 25

There'll be no funeral at Tecate, Mr. Diaz says. Some people came from San Carlos and took him away.

June 26

All day I've had a horrible suspicion that it was Mr. Diaz who turned Ramón over to the Immigration officers.

76

June 28

This was the first day I've been to work since Ramón's death. I think I'll feel better having something to do in the afternoons. Mother thinks so, too. But I'd like to give up school.

July 1

Sybil has the Blazer back again, and we went for a ride and stopped by McDonald's for hamburgers and fries. It was nice to see her again. She was shocked to hear about Ramón. We got to talking and she asked me if I had any suspicions about who reported Ramón to Immigration. I said that for a while I thought it was Mr. Diaz but I didn't think so now.

"Somebody must have," Sybil said.

"Not necessarily," I said. "They pick up aliens all the time. By the busload, Mr. Diaz tells me."

"Did your mother like Ramón?"

I lied. "I don't know whether she did or didn't. Why?"

"I was just wondering. You don't suppose it could be your mother, do you?"

I stared at her.

"It's the sort of thing *my* mother would do," Sybil said. "And mothers are all alike, if you ask me."

July 2

Today I've been thinking about my conversation with Sybil. She's the best friend I've ever had.

July 3

This morning at the breakfast table Mother asked me if I'd like to take a trip for a few days when summer school is over. I really don't want to go. Besides, I can't very well ask Mrs. Constable for more time off, since I've lost so many days already.

Mother has been very sympathetic through all this.

July 4

A lot of fireworks now, down the coast by the Coronado Hotel. The sky is afire. When the rockets go up and burst, they sound like corn popping. I am sad. The rockets made me feel sadder.

July 5

Last night, about one o'clock, I woke up, thinking about my conversation with Sybil at McDonald's when she asked me if I believed that Mother had given Ramón's name to Immigration. I've been thinking about it ever since. I know she wouldn't do a thing like that. At least I am pretty sure. But I'm going to find out, if I can, so the thought won't keep bugging me all the time.

July 6

Mother flew up to Los Angeles yesterday. I looked through her desk where she keeps all of her papers.

I found a bill from the telephone company that hadn't been opened and I opened it. There were five calls altogether—one to San Francisco, one to Los Angeles, one I had made to Oceanside, and two to San Ysidro.

I didn't know what I was looking for, and I don't know now. I put the bill back. There were some other papers lying around, but I was sort of ashamed of myself and anyway I had to go to work, so I quit poking around.

July 8

Mother is home and she brought me a present— a beautiful I. Magnin scarf. I had planned to ask her if she thought that someone had turned Ramón's name over to Immigration. But I didn't —with the scarf and her being tired, glad to be home, and everything.

July 9

Sybil and I went to an early movie tonight and had hamburgers afterward. (I paid for the works, since I've been sponging on her a lot lately.)

The news is that she's planning to take off any day now. She's just waiting for her next allowance. She doesn't know where she's going, exactly. But the biggest news is that she wants me to go along. She says that we might go to Baja California for a week or two. Maybe more.

"On the way, we could stop at San Carlos," she said.

I knew what she meant, but I didn't say anything. I tried to but I couldn't.

She asked me if I had talked to my mother about the Immigration thing and I said, no, I hadn't. I don't know why it came to me at that moment, but I remembered the two calls to San Ysidro. When I got home I looked up the numbers in the phone book, the two I'd found on the bill. Sure enough, they were made to Immigration headquarters.

July 10

This morning Mother was pouring her first cup of coffee. I sat down at the kitchen table and started to drink my orange juice. It didn't taste good. I shoved it away and looked up at my mother, sitting across from me. I didn't mean to say anything, not right then, not what I did say, but the words came spilling out.

"Mother," I said, "did you tell the Immigration officers about Ramón?"

She swallowed her mouthful of coffee, put the cup down, and wiped her mouth on the blue paper napkin. She was surprised, but she tried not to show it. She didn't answer my question directly.

"What would you have done?" she asked, but didn't wait for me to answer. "Here's a young man who comes into the country illegally. He

81

comes from where? From what? From what sort of family? He can't speak our language. He is a Catholic and seventeen years old. He has a job cutting grass, with no prospects of ever doing anything else. On the other hand, you . . ."

Mother got up and poured herself another cup of coffee and sat down and looked out the window. Then she went on.

"How in the world was I to know that Ramón would get mixed up in a shooting accident? It's terrible this had to happen. It's awful. But you must remember, Kathleen, that all I did, all of it, everything . . ."

"You never liked Ramón," I broke in. "You never would have let us marry. Would you?"

"I didn't know Ramón. He was never in this house. You never brought him here."

"Because you'd have made him feel uncomfortable. You were against us getting married all the time. From the first. Weren't you?"

"At seventeen? With you in high school and him cutting grass? I've told you all that before. A year from now things might have been different."

"Yes, they might," I said. "But now they *are* different."

Mother got up, washed out her coffee cup, and wiped it. Her hand must have been shaking because the cup rattled when she put it away in the cupboard. She went on talking for a while, but I wasn't listening.

It's late now and the foghorn is blowing.

I would like to read Mother's diary and learn what she really thinks. In case she put it down. And I would, if I could find the key to the locked drawer. She writes in her diary whether anything has happened or not. She even writes when she goes on a trip, like the one to Hawaii. We'd come in pooped out after a hard day of sightseeing. I'd flop into bed, but not Mother. She'd sit up for an hour or more, putting things down.

Why does she lock her diary up every night? Why is she so secretive? I guess for the same reason I am. How would it be if we lived in a world where no one had secrets?

Mother is in her room now. She's sitting at her folding desk, putting down what I said and what she said, etc. I wonder if she's writing the truth. I try to tell the truth in my diary. Not writing the truth is like cheating when you're playing solitaire. But then maybe you don't put down the truth always. Maybe you don't know what the truth is and what it isn't. You can do something and think you know why you did it. But maybe you don't.

Mother has finished writing. I hear her close the desk. She's walking over to the locked drawer. She's opening it now, putting her diary away. And now the key. People are locked drawers, full of secrets. With keys that are hidden away.

I don't care what Mother has written down. The truth is, she betrayed me.

Part II

This morning a hot mist covers the bay, the islands, and the long stretch of the coast. The sun is up but casts only a pearly shadow upon the cliffs and the quiet palm trees.

I start the fire under the coffee at 6:55. There is still time to waken Kathleen for school. She worked on her math until nearly midnight; an extra ten minutes of sleep seems a good idea.

The lazy sound of seven bells striking the hour drifts up from the bay. The bells come from the Coast Guard cutter *Poseidon*. My watch reads one minute after seven, and I set it back to seven. The watch is gaining a minute a day (but that isn't bad for a watch given to me on my graduation from high school more than twenty years ago).

I made a pan of blueberry muffins yesterday afternoon, the kind that comes in cartons already mixed, and all one has to do is to pour the batter into a tin. Kathleen always eats her lunch at the school cafeteria, but I wrap two of the muffins

in foil and put them in her bag to take along.
Then I squeeze three oranges, leaving in the pulp.

We plan to have waffles one morning and
omelets the next. This is omelet morning.

I open the door that leads down two steps to my
small herb garden. The wind usually blows from
this direction, from the west, but this morning it is
coming down from the Little Colorado and the
Lagunas.

I pick a few sprigs of chives for the omelet and
stand for a moment looking down upon the bay.

The foghorn on Point Loma is groaning away
like a wounded lion, groaning and catching its
breath and groaning again. The red running light
of an outgoing ship shows dimly through the mist,
and as it rounds the point I think that I hear the
sound of its bow striking the first of the Pacific
swells.

It feels good, being in a warm, safe kitchen. I
always like these mornings with the horn blowing on the headland and the lighthouse flashing.
Being safe while others grope through the fog.
It is selfish of me to feel this way, I know, but I
must confess that I enjoy it.

I go back to the kitchen, chop up the chives,
and drop them into the beaten eggs. Then I go
along the hall to the back of the house and call my
daughter. There is no answer. I call again. Still
there's no answer. I knock on the door and slowly
open it.

The first thing I see is a slight billowing movement of the white window curtains. The window is up and the open door has created a draft that is sucking the curtains in and out.

I glance toward the bed. Kathleen's long-legged doll, left over from her younger days, sits propped against a pillow. The comforter lies neatly folded. The bed is made, and this strikes me as strange; Kathleen, as long as I can remember, has never made her bed before she went to school.

The bathroom door is closed, and when I knock and get no answer, I open the door and look in. The bathroom is empty. I go back and feel the sheets. They are cold.

For what seems a long time, but must be only a moment or two, I standing staring down at the bed. Then the curtains billow a little more and I see that both the window and the screen are half open, open enough for someone to have crawled through.

I run across the room and fling them open. In the grass below me are faint footprints. They move away from the window, across the lawn in the direction of the street. They are small in the wet grass.

I think that I closed the screen and tried to lock the window. I do remember sitting down on the bed and staring at the wall. I wanted to scream, to get up and run screaming through the house, but I sat still and stared at the wall.

I couldn't move. Then I found that I could.

I jump up and go into my daughter's closet and

turn on the light. Both of Kathleen's sweaters are gone as well as three pairs of her slacks. The suitcase I had bought for her when we went to Yosemite Valley is gone. I pick up one of her dresses that has fallen on the floor and put it back on a hanger.

From far off comes the sound of the foghorn, and a wan beam of light from Point Loma moves slowly across the floor. Only then, only then, do I scream.

I feel calm when I go to the telephone and dial the office at Kathleen's school. The line is busy. I wait, counting the seconds, watching the second hand move around the dial, noticing for the first time in my life that it doesn't sweep but stumbles along in tiny jerks. I dial twice again, get busy signals, call the operator, am told in a pleasant voice suggesting patience that the line is in order.

The school is less than a half-mile away and the visibility is near zero, but I get the car started, turn on the lights, and head into the fog. I pass a line of cautious drivers, two of whom honk angrily at me, speed through a yellow light that I think is green, and double-park in the school driveway.

When I walk into the office the woman at the desk is yawning, holding her hand over her mouth. I don't want to tell her that my daughter has run away from home; she might be sitting there in class at this very moment. Instead, I simply introduce myself and ask for Kathleen Winters.

The clerk is gone a long time. The phone rings

and I am tempted to answer it. Through the window I see a girl run across the lawn, her blond hair streaming behind her. She has hair like Kathleen's, the same dark blond color of honey in the sunlight. The girl drops a book, stoops to pick it up, and glances up at the office window as she does so. It is not Kathleen.

Then I sit down and after a moment get up and go to the door that opens into the hallway. I stand there until the woman comes back. "Your daughter is not in school today," she said. Her voice sounds carefree, but perhaps it isn't.

At this moment for some reason I remember that my class, my own summer class in English II, is gathering in a schoolroom four miles away, raising hell, no doubt, waiting for their dear teacher, Sara Winters, for me.

At home, after I have arranged for a substitute, I wonder if I should call the police. Should I talk to my lawyer, John Watkins? Should I sit down quietly and gather my thoughts? It is possible after all that Kathleen has not run away. It is possible that she has run away but will decide before the day is over to come home. Anything is possible.

As soon as I open the door, I call her name. There is no answer. I go down the hall, calling again. Then the phone rings and I run into the kitchen. It's a girl, a young girl, asking for somebody or other.

"What number do you want?" I ask.

There is an instant of silence, a click as the phone goes dead. No answer, not even an apology. Our young can be heedless.

I sit down on the arm of the sofa, drink half a cup of coffee, and decide to call Mrs. Langley.

She is eating her breakfast, the maid says, but I inform her that it is an emergency call. It is quite possible, I think while I wait for her to come to the phone, that her daughter and Kathleen might have gone off together.

I am right, for as soon as I start to tell her about the events of the morning she breaks in.

"The maid," she says, "has just reported that she saw Sybil drive out at dawn."

"Kathleen must be with her," I said.

"Likely."

I can hear Mrs. Langley swallowing a mouthful of coffee.

"What should we do?" I ask. "We . . ."

"Let them have their joyride," says Mrs. Langley. "About once a year, since she was fourteen, Sybil has taken off."

"Kathleen has never done anything like this before," I say.

"Don't worry, Mrs. Winters; she's in good hands. Sybil is responsible." Mrs. Langley laughs. "Responsible in an irresponsible way, you might say. In a day or two she always comes back, full of wild tales, most of them untrue. She loves adventure. Why not?"

I interrupt her. "What if they don't come back?"

"Don't worry. When they run out of money and clean clothes and need a hot bath, they'll show up."

"But if they don't? If something should happen?"

Mrs. Langley pauses for another sip of coffee. "I'm never worried about Sybil coming back. She always has and always will. Until she gets married, that is. She likes her comfort too much."

"They may plan to come back," I say, "but something could happen."

"True. Something may. And it may happen right here in this house. In your house. On the street. At school. In Point Loma as well as in Tijuana or Timbuctu."

Mrs. Langley pauses to give the maid instructions about changing the linen in the guest room.

"But if they don't come home," I persist, "and something does happen to them . . ."

"If it does, let them take the consequences. They are old enough to be responsible for their actions. If they get into trouble, let them get out. If they're arrested, let them go to jail. If Sybil would call me now and say, 'Mother, I am in jail and I want you to come down and put up bail money for me,' I would say, 'Sybil, you got yourself into trouble, now get yourself out.' I believe that if you want to dance you must put a coin in the juke box. My daughter has had what she's wanted, within reason. I let her have the things I wanted as a girl and never had. I've taught her to know what's wrong and what's right. By now she should be old enough to keep out of trouble; if she doesn't, that's her fault."

"Kathleen is very young," I say. "She's not been raised as you have raised your daughter."

"I gather as much."

I am becoming desperate, but I really don't mean to say what I say next.

"I think I'll call the police. They'll know what to do."

Mrs. Langley explodes. "For God's sake, don't! It'll be all over town, in the papers, on radio and TV, everywhere."

July 12

I keep the lights on all night. This morning I am up at daylight and weed the garden, which doesn't need the care. At nine o'clock I call John Watkins. He is calm. As the father of six children, four of them girls, he needs to be. Trying to calm myself, I tell him about Kathleen.

"Did she leave a note?" he asks.

"No. At least I haven't found one."

"Did you call anyone besides Mrs. Langley?"

"I haven't because I don't want it to get around."

"But it will, no matter what you do. Call the police. Wait, I'll get the number for you."

Mr. Watkins is still calm. I can see him taking a cigar out of his desk, looking to see which end to snip, then snipping it with his little gold cutter, putting the cigar in his mouth and rolling it around, wetting it with his tongue, twirling the knob of his lighter and puffing, puffing until the end glows red, now looking in the phone book.

He is gone a long time before he comes back with the police number. "I'd call them now," John says. "Time is of the essence. They may still be in San Diego, just cruising around."

I put the number down, wondering how I could ever get up the nerve to use it.

"Can you call?" I ask him.

"I can," John says, "but the police will have questions that I won't be able to answer. In fact, it may be better if you go down to the station. I'll go with you, if you want me to."

"I'll phone," I say.

But I don't. I sit down in the kitchen and stare out at the empty street and the gray shadow of the misty bay beyond. I sit for more than an hour. Then I get up and unlock the front door, thinking that when Kathleen comes back, she won't have to use her key, which she always has to search for.

Deep down, I still believe that she will come back by nightfall. Surely by then.

July 13

My watch says five minutes to ten; the radio-clock in the bedroom two minutes to ten. The marine clock in the kitchen is striking the hour of ten, exactly, four deep drawn-out bells. It doesn't matter what the clocks and watches say. Time is my own, inside me.

The fog is thinning out. Off to the west where it has lifted the sky is covered with a layer of velo clouds. The clouds show up every year beginning in May and hang around until August and sometimes later, though about noon every day the sun burns them off. Tourists complain about the clouds and the cold summers. What they should do is to come later in the year after the velos have disappeared.

A family of tourists, a mother and father and two daughters, are trudging along the street, on their way to the lighthouse. One of the girls appears to be Kathleen's age. She is carrying a camera and seems happy about everything.

The light on Point Loma has gone out, but the foghorn is moaning again. It sounds different now. It no longer gives me comfort. I put my fingers in my ears, sit staring at the number John Watkins gave me. By calling the police I will admit to myself that I have given up hope that Kathleen has only wandered off somewhere.

I go into Kathleen's room and take out everything in her closet, clothes and shoes and bags, and lay all the items on the bed. I empty the bureau drawers. The last thing I come upon is the blue velvet box that holds a necklace I gave her at Christmas.

The lid is so tight I break a fingernail trying to get it open. The necklace is gone. In its place is a packet of white tissue paper folded in the shape of a triangle. I open it and find a pinch or two of small chips. I pick out one of the chips and put it in the palm of my hand. It's a hideous shade of red.

For a moment I don't know what it is. Then I remember that walking in unannounced once when Kathleen was cutting her nails, I saw her pick up the parings and put them on top of the bureau. I scooped them up as I started to clean the room.

"What are you doing?" Kathleen asked.

"Throwing these away," I said, holding out the parings.

"Don't," Kathleen said.

I stood there with the parings in one hand and the wastebasket in the other, looking at my daughter, trying to imagine why she wanted them.

"They're mine," she said.

"What are they for?"

"I haven't decided. Sybil's saving hers."

"Do you have to do everything Sybil does?"

"You don't approve?"

"I think it's silly to save fingernails. Your own."

"Whose should I save?"

"No one's. What possible good are they?"

"We have a club."

"A club that saves fingernails?"

"You make it sound silly. And it isn't."

"Who belongs to the fingernail club other than Sybil Langley?" I inquired.

"It's secret."

"A secret club? I thought that secret clubs were illegal in high school."

Kathleen opened her book and began to read.

"What do you call your club?" I asked.

Kathleen didn't look up from her book. "We don't have a name."

"I'd think a name would be hard to find."

"It's different from what you think. It's not silly. Fingernails have a significance. They're not just fingernails; they're symbols."

"Symbols of what?"

"Of the person. Of the person herself and how lasting and indestructible and different each person is."

"I see," I commented, though I didn't see at all.

"Fingernails are like fingerprints," Kathleen said. "No two are alike. Everyone's is different from everyone else's."

I put the parings back on the bureau and nothing more was said, but Kathleen must have gone on saving them because there are many more now than on that Saturday morning in the spring.

I search the room for her diary. She had wanted a diary for Christmas and I had given her a good one, book-size with a leather binding and her name in gold letters. I search everywhere, even under the rug, under the bed, but apparently she has taken it with her.

I close the door and go back to the front room, where I can watch the street, people coming and going.

I don't remember much about the rest of the day except that I stopped breathing every time I heard a car go by or someone walking on the street or a voice.

Evening comes and beams from the lighthouse sweep the horizon, showing red then white, then, after a long interval, red again. As I sit here watching the light, I feel for the first time that Kathleen is not coming home.

July 14

At suppertime I call Linda Sanders. Linda and Kathleen have been cool to each other for months. Something has happened, some difference that neither of them will talk about; I don't expect to learn much.

Instead of Linda I get her mother. Mrs. Sanders is a bright, nervous young woman who talks a lot and never seems to listen when you talk. After a few words I ask for her daughter and am told that she hasn't come home. Then Mrs. Sanders wants to chat, but I excuse myself and hang up with the guilty feeling that she knows something is wrong.

Within a few minutes Linda comes to the door. I have always liked her and I was sorry when she and Kathleen had a falling out. She stands in the doorway, looking at me, trying to smile. She knows about Kathleen.

"Mother told me you called," she says. "Are you worried? I know you are. I am, too."

"I'm terribly worried."

"Do you want me to tell you what I heard? The girls were talking in front of the school and one of them said that Kathleen and Sybil have hit the road. Those were the words they used. They have hit the road. They went in Sybil's Blazer. It belongs to Sybil's father, but she took it anyway. They left this morning, early. At dawn."

I ask Linda to sit down.

"I can't," she says, "but I'll come back. I'll be by on my way to school in the morning."

"Did you hear anything else?"

"Nothing, Mrs. Winters."

"Where do you think they can be?"

"I don't know. Honestly, I don't know."

"Where would *you* go if you ran away?"

Linda pushes her fingers through her hair. "I never thought about it."

"If you did think about it, where would you go?"

"Some place that's glamorous, I guess. Like Hollywood, maybe."

"Tijuana?"

"I don't think so. No, not there. But Hollywood. Or San Francisco, maybe."

"The girl Kathleen left with, Sybil Langley."

"I don't know her very well, Mrs. Winters. She's a new girl here. I'm not even sure where she lives. I've got to leave now."

I turn on the porch light and the light in the driveway and check to see that the front door and the back door are unlocked. I make myself a cup of broth but don't drink it. It sits here.

July 15

Linda, true to her word, comes by on her way to school. In her arms are two thick books. I hold the door open and she comes in but sees by my face that I have heard nothing. There isn't much to say, and she leaves.

I watch her walk to the corner and get on the bus, the same bus that has picked Kathleen up for the past two years. I wait until the bus lumbers away. Then I go to the phone, call the police, am

101

told that it will help matters if I report my information in person to headquarters in San Diego. Twenty minutes later I am there.

The sergeant is young; young enough to be my son. (They say you are growing old when the policemen look young.) He would have looked even younger without the Fu Manchu mustache.

I have brought two pictures of Kathleen, taken within the last year. The sergeant examines both of them.

"They could be different girls. Which comes the closest?"

"The Polaroid."

"Her hair?"

"She's blond."

"Eyes?"

"Dark brown."

"Age?"

"Kathleen will be sixteen next month."

"Height?"

"About five feet, eight inches."

"Tall."

"Yes, tall and slender."

I feel strange, standing there describing my daughter to a young man, a boy with pencil and pad and a drooping mustache. This is happening to someone else, I think, not to Sara Winters.

"Any distinguishing features? Unusual ways of walking, dressing, speech? Anything like that?"

"None that I can think of, except that sometimes when she's excited she stutters a little."

For some reason the sergeant doesn't comment on this nor put it down on his pad.

"You're married?" he asks.

"My husband is dead."

"Any relatives she might visit?"

"Some in the South, but Kathleen doesn't know them very well."

"Did your daughter leave a note?"

"No."

"Any reasons for her running away? Arguments?"

"None," I say, hearing, as I answer him, Kathleen's voice and my own, our words about Ramón. "None."

"Trouble in school? Fight with a boyfriend?"

"No."

The sergeant fills out a blank form and has me sign it. The card gives me the right, the sergeant explains, to seize my daughter. Without it I won't have the right to touch her, to bring her home.

I am no sooner in the house than the sergeant calls to tell me that a girl has been detained who answers some parts of Kathleen's description.

"Does your daughter," he asks me, "have a tattoo mark between her thumb and forefinger? A dot?"

"No."

"Does she have a gold filling in a front tooth? A large one?"

"No."

"By the way, have you thought of offering a

reward? It might make the difference between finding your daughter and not finding her."

"How much of a reward?"

"How much can you afford?"

"I can't afford anything. But if it means my daughter . . ."

"How does a thousand strike you?"

"I think I can get that together. When is it needed?"

"As soon as we announce. The sooner the better."

"It will take me a day or two. Maybe I can have it tomorrow."

"Tomorrow, good. I'll call if anything turns up. There are lots of runaway girls on the streets. A couple of thousand here in San Diego. About twelve thousand in New York. About five hundred thousand running around between here and there. We're locating some every day. The reward will help a lot. People talk when they smell money."

July 16

Linda comes by as soon as school is out. I am sitting at the kitchen table, trying to figure out how to raise a thousand dollars. In one hand she holds a sad little flower that she has picked up somewhere. I put it in a vase and we stand in the middle of the floor, looking at each other. "I didn't hear any real news," Linda says. "Nothing new."

"There's not much to hear, I guess."

"But the girls *were* talking.

"There are a lot of rumors. Susan Lee said she heard that someone had seen Sybil's car in Tijuana. It's yellow with a picture on the back. A painted picture of a mountain and a lake and a deer standing beside the lake."

Linda brushes her hair back with the side of her hand and waits for me to say something. Though I search, I can't find my thoughts. The sound of a ship's horn drifts up from the bay, one long quavering blast. The sound fades away but leaves an uneasy quiet in its wake.

Linda goes over and picks up one of the books she had put down when she came in. "I wonder, Mrs. Winters, if you could help me with my grammar. I'm having trouble. I asked my mother to help but she joked about it. She said that the day the teacher passed out grammar she was playing left field on the softball team."

"I'll try."

"Now?"

"Now is good."

We sit down at the kitchen table, the two of us, side by side, and start to work on her next day's lesson.

Before we are through, Mrs. Sanders, who is jealous of her daughter, calls and asks if Linda is there and if she is for me to send her home at once. "Linda can be a nuisance, you know," she says. I get the impression that she is annoyed with both of us, with me more than with her daughter. Linda has probably told her that she was going to ask me to help with her grammar.

When I give Linda her mother's message, she gathers up her books. "Mother's always on my back," she says. "You didn't keep after Kathleen like that, did you?"

"Sometimes."

"You asked me yesterday if I'd ever thought of running away. And I said that I hadn't. But right at this minute, I *am* thinking about it."

I look at her, wondering if secretly she doesn't admire Kathleen for what she's done.

She stands in the doorway, hesitating, as if she wants to say something to make me feel better, something sympathetic about Kathleen.

"You and Kathleen," I say, "had a falling out. What was it? I'd like to know."

"It just happened."

"Over what?"

"Over brownies."

"Brownies?"

"Cookies. Chocolate cookies with hash mixed in."

"I never heard of them."

"Neither did I until the day in cooking class."

The phone rings, and as I pick it up I hear sounds of someone breathing. Then the phone clicks and goes dead.

Linda is halfway out the door, holding her books

under one arm. "The whole class was making brownies," she says." I was standing at the counter next to Sybil. She took something out of the front of her dress—it looked like brown powder—and dropped it into the mixing bowl with the dough. I asked her what it was, and she didn't answer and went on mixing the dough. When the brownies were done, she divided them up and gave one to Susan and one to Kathleen and one to me. I took a bite of mine and it tasted sort of funny—not bad but funny—and I asked Sybil what she'd put into it.

"'Hash, dummy,' she said. 'Hash. Eat. You'll like it.'

"Kathleen and Susan ate theirs but I was afraid, so I told Sybil that I'd eat mine later. This made her mad. She called me chicken and told me not to say anything to anybody. 'You know what happens to ratfinks,' she said. She never spoke to me after that."

July 17

I borrow a thousand dollars as soon as the bank opens and get a certified check—the manager doesn't ask why I want the money—and take the check down to Sergeant Williams at the police station. I feel better now, knowing that other people will be helping, the police and others too.

The phone rings at nine in the morning, one day after I have posted the reward.

It rings twice before I can get to it, and as I pick up the receiver there's a click and for a moment I think that whoever was on the line has hung up. But after I say hello twice, I hear a faint voice at the other end.

"Hello," I say again. The voice grows strong, as if it is coming closer. I have the feeling that I have heard it before. It sounds like Mr. Herman, who sells fish down at the wharf and who is small with a voice twice as big as he is.

"Mrs. Winters?"

"Yes. Who is this?"

"My name isn't important."

"Yes."

"You don't know me."

"Yes."

"Do you have a daughter about sixteen years old, with blond hair, by the name of Kathleen?"

"Yes."

The voice still sounds as if it belonged to Mr. Herman. I can visualize him as the man goes on talking. He is standing behind the counter with a long knife in his white hands, slicing up a piece of swordfish.

"Did you post a reward?" the caller asks.

"For information . . ."

The voice breaks in. "A reward of one thousand?"

"For information . . ."

"One thousand?"

"Yes."

In the background, in the silence before the man goes on, I can hear people talking. Then I hear a guitar and someone singing a word or two in Spanish.

"Where is she?" I ask.

"I'll come to that," the caller answers.

I wait. Whoever it is must be holding his hand over the receiver because I can't hear the sounds I heard before. I wait for a long time; then I hear a faint stirring that sounds like someone breathing.

"Hello, hello," I say. "Are you on the phone?"

"Yes, I'm here. I had to attend to a matter. Sorry. I'm ready to talk."

I can hear the guitar again and the voices.

The caller says, "First, about the thousand. You'll have to up it, Mrs. Winters."

"Has Kathleen been kidnaped?"

"Nothing like that. It's complicated, though. Very complicated."

"Is she in danger?"

"No. Everything's in shape."

"What do you want me to do?"

"First, there's the matter of money."

109

"I work for a living."

"You won't need much."

"How much?"

"Three thousand."

"How can I get so much money?"

"Remember, lady, it's your *daughter* we're talking about."

"Where is she?"

"We'll talk about that later."

I hear music again, the breathing, the voices. The man could be calling from a bar or a café.

"Where are you?" I ask.

"In Mexico," the caller says. "In Tijuana."

"What am I to do now?"

"Get the money."

"I'll try."

"Try hard, Mrs. Winters. You can cancel the reward. Then you'll only have to raise two thousand. It's about ten after nine now. I'll call you again at noon. Exactly. And no monkey business. This isn't a snatch, madam. Your daughter isn't gagged and locked up. Keep your mouth shut and don't talk to the police. Get the money in cash, half in twenties, half in fifties. I'll call you back at noon."

I wait a few minutes after the man hangs up and then phone John Watkins.

"It sounds as if you're mixed up with a crazy," he says. "I'd call the police and not waste time about it."

"I was warned against that."

"I'd call anyway."

110.

"I was told to keep my mouth shut."

"Well, you haven't. You're talking to me."

I leave it at that and hang up, feeling that I can expect little from John Watkins. Should I believe the caller, whoever he may be? Does he really know where Kathleen is? Can he return her to me? Or will he take my money and do nothing? And the money itself? How can I raise another $2000?

I am confused. I haven't made up my mind about anything when the phone rings again, exactly at noon.

The caller says, "You have the money?"

"I'll get it," I say.

"Three thousand; half in twenties, the rest in fifties. And all of it unmarked. Put the money in a flight bag, the kind you buy at the airport, a blue bag with a handle. What sort of car do you drive?"

"A nineteen seventy-four Pinto, green," I say, and I give him the license number. I know that he writes the number down because he asks me to wait a moment while he finds a pencil.

"You still there?" he asks.

"I'm here."

"Now listen. Cross the border tonight at seven forty-five. Come alone in your car. And don't have anyone follow, like a friend or a cop. You putting this down?"

I am not putting it down, trusting my good memory. "Yes," I answer.

"No one follows you, Mrs. Winters. That's important. You've been to Tijuana before?"

"Yes."

"Good. After you leave Mexican customs, keep right across the aqueduct to the main street. Turn left. When you get to the second corner, turn right to the auto park in the middle of the block. Park and walk back to the main street. And don't forget the bag with the twenties and fifties.

"Walk three blocks, you come to the Gatito Café. Two entrances. Use the one around the corner, not the one on the main street. You'll see a bar on the opposite side of the room, past the dance floor. There won't be any dancing at that hour. Cross the dance floor and go to the far end of the bar. That's the end on your right. You'll see a small table. Put the bag on the floor under the table and leave the way you came in.

"Go to the Hotel Valencia, back down the street across from where you parked. A room's reserved for you. Go to the room and wait. Your daughter will show up. Around eleven maybe."

I am writing down the instructions now, no longer trusting my memory.

"Remember, Mrs. Winters, the deal's off if you bring the cops. Follow the instructions the way I gave them and by this time tomorrow you'll be home safe, with your daughter. Any questions?"

"None, but I am not thinking clearly."

"You might be thinking that this is a put-on.

You might be tempted to do something silly. Like telling your friends or the law."

"Everything you say makes it sound as if my daughter has been kidnaped."

"Like I told you once, she's safe, walking around in Tijuana at this moment."

"I also think that you might be making all this up. How do I know that you've ever seen my daughter?"

There's a pause. "Is your daughter a tall blonde with brown eyes?" he asks. "Hair brushed back from her forehead?"

"You could get that much from the description I gave the police."

"Does your daughter stutter sometimes?"

"Yes."

"Does she wear four rings, two of them on each hand? All of them some sort of green stones? Also one with a pearl in it."

There is no doubt now that he has seen my daughter.

"What is your name?" I say.

"Just think of me as a guy named Joe. And that could be all right. My name might be Joe. By the way, Mrs. Winters, how about a description of yourself?"

"I am of medium height and weight. About one hundred and thirty pounds. My hair is brown with some gray in it and I wear it in back in a twist."

"Ribbons? Combs?"

"No."

"What'll you wear?"

I think. "A blue dress and a white sweater."

"I'll know you. Now do not, repeat, do not bring loving friends or nosy cops."

There's a pause. Then I hear sounds in the background again—a guitar, voice, a small dog barking.

"By the way," the caller says, "don't forget to bring the identification card, the police card, that gives you the right to seize your daughter. You've got one?"

"Yes, I have it."

"And something else, lady. Just in case you have second thoughts about the matter. Mexican police are known to frame runaway kids, especially girls, send them to prison on trumped-up charges. Mexican prisons are expensive, especially if you want your daughter to have a bed to sleep in and something fit to eat."

At two o'clock I go to the bank and ask the manager for a new loan on my house. He reminds me that I have just paid off my first loan, but the papers are ready to sign ten minutes later. I have no trouble getting the twenty- and fifty-dollar bills, although the teller does give me a curious look before he counts out the money, as if the money belongs to him.

The airport is on the way to the bank, so I have the flight bag with me, a blue one with a handle. I leave the bag in the trunk and don't fill it until I get back to the car and make sure no one is watching.

I return to the house, sit down, and try to think. I think of going to Tijuana without the money, of walking into the Gatito Café and looking around, perhaps sitting at the bar for a while. It is possible that I may see the man I had talked to. I am certain that I will know his voice if I hear it again.

I go back and forth, from one idea to another, finally deciding to take the money with me, park the car in a garage on the U.S. side of the border, leave the money locked in the trunk, and take a taxi to the Gatito Café. If I need to, I can always go back for the bag.

But when I get to the border at 7:15 that night I can't find a parking place on the U.S. side that looks safe. I decide to drive into Tijuana and park the car on the main street, in a place where people are passing.

At the border the Mexican customs officer asks me where I'm from. It is just a formality. I've gone through it before. All they usually want to know is whether you speak English. But this time he stops me and asks if I have any bags in the car. I point to the blue flight bag on the seat beside me. He gives it a quick glance, smiles, and waves me on. There is something about his smile that is false.

I find a place to park in front of a drug store and lock the flight bag in the trunk. Since the sidewalk is jammed with Mexicans and tourists, I take to the street and make my way to the Gatito Café. It is exactly 7:45 when I arrive.

A barker stands beside the main entrance, dressed in a fancy charro outfit, flaring pants, a short jacket covered with sequins, and an outsize sombrero. As the caller has instructed me to do, I take the side entrance and find myself in a room that at some time or other could have been a garage. It is fitted out with a dance floor, three revolving juke boxes, a ceiling festooned with a thousand colored ribbons, and a long bar. A few customers are sitting up front.

I take a stool at the far end of the bar. I don't want a drink, but I order one anyway. The bartender is not the man who called me.

When the drink comes, in a tall glass with three straws, each in a different color, the bartender leaves beside the check a folded note. It is written in a cramped hand and reads, "Where is the blue bag? Don't fool around."

I take a sip of the drink, go out into the street, fight my way against the crowd back to the car, and take the bag out of the trunk. I do all this in a hurry. But once I have the bag in my hand I pause and take a deep breath.

Not more than ten paces away are two policemen. They are watching me, looking at the blue flight bag but pretending not to. I remember that the guard had glanced at the bag when I crossed the border an hour earlier. It occurs to me that there may be some connection between the guard and the policemen; that all three have an interest in the money I'm carrying.

I get in the car, lock the doors, and in my mind go back over each step I have taken that day, since the moment I decided to follow the caller's instructions. I try to be calm and to think clearly. I do neither. I am in a panic, a quiet, orderly panic if there is such a thing. Am I being foolish? Should I have taken John Watkins's advice and told the police about the telephone calls? If Kathleen is in Tijuana, and I feel that she is, it might be possible to find her myself.

The policemen have moved off a step or two but are still watching. I decide to drive up the street and park in a different location. The traffic is heavy; I have trouble finding a place; and in desperation finally pull into a parking lot. I sit there with the doors locked for a long time, for twenty minutes anyway. The policemen haven't followed me; at least they're not visible.

Bells in a nearby church are ringing as I get out of the car. A friendly note. Winding the flight bag's strap twice around my wrist, I start up the crowded street. It's a hot night, and I am covered with sweat before I go far. I am not aware of being followed.

The Gatito Café is close, on the other side of the street and half a block away, but there is still time for me to change my mind. To get myself back across the border and home. To wait there for another call. Meanwhile to think, to think hard about what I am engaged in. One thing I have decided: I'll not call the police and divulge what I know. But I make my way toward the Gatito, clutching the flight bag, knowing underneath, in the back of my mind, that I will go into the café and sit at the bar.

The Gatito is filling up. The three juke boxes revolve in a blaze of light, playing different tunes. I find the stool I sat on before. My unfinished drink with the three colored straws is still on the bar. The penciled note is gone. I order a new drink from a bartender I didn't see the first time. He brings it, without straws this time and without a note. I pay for my drink and sit holding the bag in my lap, the canvas handle still wound around my wrist.

I sip my drink and order another. I sit there for an hour. It is now twenty minutes to ten. I go outside and up the street, carrying the bag. At the last minute I've decided not to leave it behind, under the table, which is only an arm's length away.

The Valencia is a hotel without an elevator. My room is on the third floor and the stairs are steep and I arrive there, out of breath, to find it a cubicle, with no closet, one window, a single bulb hanging overhead.

I turn on the light, open the window, and sit down where I can look into the street. The side-

walks are still filled with tourists; cars are streaming past.

I sit here for an hour. It is now eleven o'clock,
the hour designated by Joe, the caller. I get up
and open the door; then decide to close and bolt
it. I hear footsteps on the stairs, loud voices in the
hallway. They come and disappear. I wait until
midnight, and then pick up the bag and go down-
stairs and into the street.

The Gatito is on fire with colored lights, explod-
ing with rock music. I circle the dance floor, edg-
ing my way toward the bar. As the music stops
and the dancers leave the floor, I catch sight of a
girl standing by one of the juke boxes. She is wearing a long Mexican dress and a wide-brimmed,
silver-spangled sombrero.

The girl turns toward me, and as she does so,
as she stands with clouds of the night's cigarette
smoke swirling around her, I see that it is Kathleen.

I call her name and start toward her across the
crowded floor.

She can't hear me above the bedlam of voices
and music. Again, with all the breath I can find, I
call her name.

Dancers are pouring onto the floor. A drunk
grabs my arm. I push my way into the streaming
mass, suddenly stumble, clumsily regain my bal-
ance. Somehow I reach the juke box where Kathleen was standing. She is no longer there.

I search for her until the crowd thins out and

I am certain she has gone. Then I return to the hotel and sit by the window. Lights are still flashing along the street, as bright and gaudy as they were hours before. A cold mist blows in from the sea, shrouding everything.

The rest of the night I sit by the open window, afraid to leave the room. At dawn, when my daughter hasn't come, I take the bag and walk past the Gatito Café. It is closed and shuttered, the sidewalk littered with beer cans, discarded mementos of the night.

Fog is rolling through the streets as I drive to the border.

Appearing suddenly out of the fog, the customs officer wants to know if I have bought anything in Mexico. I shake my head. As he pokes around in the back seat, glances at the flight bag, and finally orders me to open the trunk, I am tempted to tell him what has happened to me. I think better of it.

I decide to drive home and wait for further word from Joe. I am sure that he will call. But questions assail me. It is possible that Kathleen heard me scream her name. It is possible. But how can she continue to doubt that what I did was done only for her health, her happiness, all the days of her future? In a year, even less, with dollars in his pocket Ramón would have taken her back to his mountain village. And there she would be, stuck for the rest of her life, having one child after the other, living like a peon.

If only I could have the chance to sit down and talk to her, to make her see that I have a responsibility, a mother's responsibility, to protect her from passing notions and desires.

July 20

A windy day, with whitecaps on the sea and small sailboats tacking back and forth in some sort of a race. While I stand at the window, the gray launch that belongs to Mr. Herman's son, who fishes in Mexican waters, chugs into the harbor, followed by a flight of hovering gulls. The boat is flying a flag, which means that it has a catch of swordfish. It reminds me that I haven't eaten a meal in two days.

Housewives along the street are already on their way to Mr. Herman's, and I join the crowd. His market is small, and cluttered with odds and ends of the sea: a mammoth stuffed swordfish, a collection of harpoons, the picture of a mermaid sitting on a rock. Upstairs are rooms where he lives with his son, who catches the fish he sells.

Mr. Herman has heard about Kathleen already. "I'd hate to try to bring a girl up these days," he says. "What with all the booze and dope and things that go on. Mine grew up and got married just in the nick of time."

"You're lucky," I say.

"That's what I tell myself."

Mr. Herman wraps a thick slice of swordfish in newspaper.

"I feel sorry," he says. "If there's anything I can do, I hope you'll give me a call."

I'm very hungry, but I decide to take time to prepare the fish properly. I preheat the oven. Even swordfish fresh from the sea dries out quickly, so I melt a generous portion of butter, wait for it to settle, then skim it, coat the broiler rack and then the steak itself with the clarified butter. I broil the fish for five minutes and baste. Then turn and baste and broil it for another five minutes. I slice a lemon, pick parsley from my garden for garnish, and sit down before the beautiful, golden brown steak. It turns my stomach. I sit there for an hour and don't touch it.

At dusk as I am looking through the window at the stormy sea and the sailboats in the harbor, the phone rings. It rings, as it always does now, in the middle of my stomach. It is Joe.

"I'm disappointed with the way things turned out," he says. "But it wasn't my fault. My instructions were for you to stay in the hotel until your daughter came, remember?"

There is a noise in the background, like a car starting up.

I wait.

"Are you there?" Joe asks.

"Yes."

"Your daughter is still in Baja," he says.

"How do you know?"

"The same way I knew before."

Silence. More voices.

"Let's try it again," the caller says. "Once more. Come tomorrow night, the same as before. And don't be stupid. Leave the money this time and stay put in the hotel, as instructed."

The phone clicks and goes dead.

I go out on the porch. The light on Point Loma begins to flash on and off, on and off. In the clear evening air its beam goes far out to sea. To the south, in Tijuana, the first lights wink and shimmer.

Kathleen, please come home!

Part III

It was just four in the morning when I slipped out of the house. I didn't leave a note because I didn't know what to say.

I went away in my bare feet. Sybil was waiting for me at the corner and we drove down to Sambo's on 101 and had breakfast. We talked until it was light and then we headed out for Tijuana and crossed the border when people were beginning to go to work.

There wasn't any trouble getting across. Sybil thought there might be. Her mother usually slept late but she just might have been prowling around earlier than usual, found the note Sybil left, and called the police.

We parked on the main street in Tijuana, right in front of the church. Sybil had everything figured out beforehand, as if she was used to running away from home, as if she ran away every month.

"The first thing," she said, "is the paint shop. When the word gets around, the San Diego police will call the Mexican police, who'll be on the look-out for a yellow seventy-seven Chevy Blazer with green stripes around the windows and a person-alized license number, NOV 1—that's my father's birthday."

We waited for eight o'clock.

People went into the church, and small mer-chants spread their wares out on the sidewalk.

A young man stood on the corner and watched us. Another man, with a tooth missing in front, who looked as if he hadn't been to bed, stuck his face in the window and wanted to know if he could help us to start a beautiful new day. Sybil answered him by rolling up the window and lock-ing the door.

At eight o'clock we drove around to the Tres Hermanas Garage.

Sybil hadn't been there before but someone had told her about it. It was owned by three sisters. One of them spoke English, and Sybil explained what she wanted. It was the $99 special kit, which included a 24-hour paint job and a false tail pipe for hiding valuables and such.

"What color do you want?" Sybil asked me. "Red?"

"Too loud. You'd see it a mile away."

"Bronze with yellow stripes and wheels?"

"Bronze with bronze wheels, O.K."

We left the Blazer and took our overnight bags and found a pretty good hotel, called the Valencia. Then we went to a printing shop in an alley be-

hind a drug store that Sybil knew about and got
I.D. cards, with new names for both of us.

My new name is Hilary Coleridge. I chose it
myself, remembering Kubla Khan. Sybil's is Mary
Lou Taliaferro. Being from New York, our resi-
dence is the Plaza Hotel. That's where Eloise
lived.

We also bought two driver's licenses, using our
new names. My age is now eighteen. I've always
wanted to be eighteen.

Everything together cost $50. Sybil paid for it
out of the $1920 she has. Where did she get all
the money? I'm broke. I'll have to get a job soon.

Why is it that when a girl leaves home, she's
called a runaway? And when a boy leaves home,
he's called an adventurer? The way I look at it,
Christopher Columbus was a runaway.

After we got our new identities and everything
we went back to the Hotel Valencia.

Sybil hadn't slept much and I hadn't slept any,
so we both turned in.

We didn't wake up until dark. We sat around
and talked and then went to a taco stand and
ate three tacos apiece. They were so hot that Sybil
drank two bottles of beer. I drank one, though I
don't like beer. My mouth is still burning.

From there we went to a place near the Jai Alai
Palace. It was a dark hole and had pictures of jai
alai players hanging on the walls and a small bar
at one end. Sybil ordered another beer and I had
a Dr Pepper.

She said something to the bartender. I think it was, "Is Sally here?" Whatever it was, he gave her an envelope with some red pills and some white ones in it. She took a red one and washed it down with beer.

She offered me one but I refused. I wanted to get things straight between us right at the start, so I told her that I wasn't going to use pot, ever. She said the pills weren't pot. They were uppers and downers, and I'd probably need one before the night was over.

We walked around for a while. Then we drifted into a big place called El Gatito Café. A thousand lights were blinking out in front. Twice that many inside.

There were a lot of tables around a dance floor, three big Wurlitzers whirling around and a bar at one end. We picked out a table near the floor. It was Sybil's idea. Sybil ordered a beer and I ordered one too, but didn't drink it.

We weren't there very long before two sailors came over. They both had pink cheeks and looked as though they'd never had to shave. They asked us for a dance. My sailor asked where I was from, how old I was, and a lot of other questions. I guess I didn't give the right answers because he drifted away after one dance. Good riddance!

The manager of the place, who wears a cowboy hat with red spangles on it, heard me speaking Spanish to the waitress and asked me if I wanted a job waiting table. Two dollars a day and tips.

Sybil thought it was a good idea, and since I am low on funds I took it.

I went to work at eight and by ten I had $11.50 in tips, mostly from sailors on the U.S.S. *Barracuda.*

There was a big show at ten, singing waitresses, two Spanish dancers, and two comedians. The manager shoved me in with the singing waitresses, and when he heard my voice on one of the high notes of "El Rancho Grande," he asked me if I would like to sing regularly. The Mexican Nightingale.

July 13

No car today. Some sort of foul-up with the phony tail pipe. But at least the car's been painted. We should have it by tomorrow, Señorita Carmen says. I asked her if the *federales* have been nosing around, and she shook her head.

The big problem is a new set of license plates. She wanted $100 for some from Tennessee, which are small and hard for the fuzz to read, but Sybil got a good pair from New York for $80.

The Blazer looks sharp, all in bronze with the orange and black license plates from the Empire State.

Sybil can't wait to get on the road. She keeps talking about Culiacán, where they grow hundreds of acres of poppies, the kind they make heroin from.

Tips today came to $21.90.

July 14

More trouble with the tail pipe, but we'll have it by tomorrow morning. "*Seguro que sí,*" Señorita Carmen says. For sure. No *federales* are hanging around, but we're both getting jittery.

Yesterday's thought was by Satchel Paige: "Don't look back. Something may be gaining on you."

At this moment, it's a good thought for Sybil and me to keep in mind.

July 15

No car.

July 16

Ditto.

July 19

It's happened. It's happened.

It was midnight, and a dance had just ended and I was getting ready to join the singers. I looked around and there, right there, was Mother. Not a dozen steps away. I ducked behind a palm and ran. I heard my name. Twice. I kept running. There was a crowd on the sidewalk. I pushed through and got into the street somehow. I lost the ribbon in my hair but I didn't stop. I ran into a dark street and circled back to the hotel.

Sybil came in about five minutes later. I was still so out of breath I couldn't talk. Sybil opened the envelope.

"Have a downer," she said. "You look like you could use one."

I took a white and swallowed it.

Last week there was a saying by someone or other: "Only he who has chaos within him can give birth to a star."

The way I feel now I can give birth to a constellation!

Sybil was up at dawn. It's funny how she goes in spurts. One day she just lies around eating and sleeping. The next day she's all over the place. I wonder if it's the the uppers and downers.

We had breakfast after we checked out. I ordered huevos rancheros, which had a lot of fierce sauce and creamy goat cheese sprinkled around over the eggs. Yum! Sybil told me to fill up because we'd probably be skipping lunch.

We went over to the Tres Hermanas Garage at seven. They were still working on the false tail pipe. The paint job's super, as though it had come right from the factory.

The Gatito owes me for a day's work, since I didn't wait to get paid last night. No wonder! I made $49 in tips, which isn't bad, considering that I'd have had to work for a week at the Turf and Surf to make as much.

While they were working on the phony tail pipe. I walked up to the cathedral. I went by a back way, down an alley, and kept an eye out.

Not being a Catholic, I didn't know what to do when I got inside. But anyway, I went down the aisle to the altar, where a lot of candles were burning. To one side were five or six rows of candles, some burning and some just sitting there in little glass cups.

A girl my age was standing beside the candles. I watched her put a copper coin in a box and take out a match. Then she lit one of the candles and knelt down and prayed. I waited until she got up and moved away, then I did everything just as she had done.

While I was on my knees, I prayed.

The stone floor was hard. I hadn't prayed for a long time, not since my father was sent home from the war and we had services for him at Point Loma in the big cemetery that belongs to the Navy. It took me a while to get my thoughts together, to quit seeing myself in a Mexican cathedral down on my knees in front of an altar burning with candles.

After a while I forgot that I was kneeling there. I did what I had come to do. I prayed for Ramón Sandoval, my dearest love.

Sybil was waiting for me, walking up and down, swinging her arms. She's still either in a hurry or half asleep. One or the other. Nothing between.

"We can make it south or north or east," she said. "Anywhere but west. The ocean's out there, a lot of it. What do you want to do?"

"It's up to you," I said.

"The fun's in Los Mochis and Culiacán. We get there by going straight east to Mexicali and then south. Above five days. Or we can head south from here to Ensenada and on to Rosalía. At Rosalía we can catch an ore ship, if they're running, or go on to La Paz and hop a ferry across the gulf to Mazatlán. It's south of Los Mochis and Culiacán. It's about the same either way."

Sybil always amazes me. Every day I find out something new about her. She makes punk grades in school. She doesn't know where the Declaration of Independence was signed or who signed it. She never heard of John Keats. But she knows what's going on out there in the big world. A world I catch glimpses of now and then. Only glimpses. The real world?

"Well?" Sybil said. She was growing impatient. "I thought you wanted to go to San Carlos and talk to Ramón's family."

"I do. I do."

"Then let's hit the road before we get picked up for loitering."

We came to a place in about an hour where there were two cafés sitting up on a bluff, a trailer park, and a white beach below.

In the window of one of the cafés was a sign, WAITRESS WANTED, so Sybil and I talked it over and decided that I'd better apply, since the bill at the paint shop had run more than she'd planned for. They gave me a Mexican sombrero and an apron and I went right to work, serving lunch.

I had five tables. All of the customers were American. I spoke Spanish to them and a few words of English. One of the men complimented me on my English. Why do a lot of men like to show off in front of their wives? See, Mildred, watch how I can turn on a girl young enough to be my granddaughter. "Señorita . . . Mildred, how do you say 'eyes' in Spanish?" If they only knew what turkeys they are!

Sybil went down to the beach and lay in the sand. After work I went down too, and we talked until it was time for me to go back.

It was a long day. Sybil gave me a red after supper, and I felt better.

At least Mother isn't following us.

The way I feel now, I am not going home for a long time. Maybe never.

July 21

I made $15 in tips today. That's $27.34 I've made altogether.

We plan to leave in the morning. We're going to Rosalía. That's a town near the place where Ramón was born and where his family lives. It's about 300 miles away, I think.

Sybil bought a few shots of heroin from the cook today. He has a lot stashed away in the icebox. He says it comes from Culiacán. I suppose that's why Sybil wants to go to Culiacán. I want to go and I don't want to. Maybe I won't think about things so much if I can see Ramón's family and talk to them.

July 22

We got an early start and went through Ensenada while the roosters were still crowing.

We were stopped at a checkpoint about fifteen miles south of there. A place called Estero. The guard wasn't much older than I am. He was sleepy, but he smiled when I spoke to him in Spanish. All he asked was, "Do you have firearms?" He didn't ask us about dope. The road was good, so we made a lot of miles before dark.

I am writing this by the light of our campfire, on the edge of what our map shows to be a big desert.

July 23

We crossed the desert today from the Pacific Ocean to the Sea of Cortez. When Conquistador Hernando Cortez saw Baja 300 years ago, he thought that it was an island. The sea looks like a big lake. As we drove along the shore I remembered what Ramón had told me.

138

"There are many white beaches," he'd said, "and bays with blue water in them."

We would see them on our honeymoon, he said.

July 24

This afternoon we came to Santa Rosalía and parked in the town square. It had a big copper mine at one time and a mill that belonged to some Frenchmen. It's closed now, but the town is still here.

The first thing Sybil found out was that the ore boat is not running. I asked a soldier in a tan uniform that was too tight for him where San Carlos was. I asked him too if he knew the Sandoval family.

"Which Sandoval?" he asked. "There are many."

"The family of Ramón."

"He that was killed by the Americans?"

"By someone."

"By the Americans, it is said."

The soldier made markings in the dust with his finger, showing us how to reach the village of San Carlos. We had missed it and must go back. But it wasn't far—about fifteen miles—at the end of a bad road, so we decided to stay all night and go in the morning.

139

Sybil is getting impatient to get going to Culiacán. By tomorrow afternoon at the latest. She's out of uppers and downers. I could use an upper myself.

July 25

I was awake at dawn. A pretty dawn. A pearly haze over the sea. The sun coming up out of the haze.

I had a hard time getting Sybil awake. She came to, but I couldn't get her on her feet. She finally managed to tell me to take the Blazer and go to San Carlos by myself.

"Remember," she said, "that you're in Mexico. If someone runs into you or you run into someone, whether it's your fault or not, the police haul you into jail. Jail here wouldn't be any fun, and it takes a lot of money to get out. I'm going down and lie on the beach. Make it short."

I'd never driven a four-wheel drive before and the family car only twice, but I got to San Carlos all right.

The road wasn't any more than a goat path. There was a store in the village, a gas pump, and a spring that flowed out of a rock and ran under the road. The man who owned the store came out with me and pointed to a house above us on a low hill.

"That is Sandoval," he said. "His son was killed by the Americans."

"I know," I told him.

There was no road, only a winding path between a ragged grove of palm trees.

Three friendly dogs came out of the house to greet me. But it really wasn't a house. It was more of a lean-to with a slanting roof of palm leaves, with a sort of *ramada*, a pergola, outside and an oven where an early fire was burning.

It all seemed familiar, as if I'd been there before. Then I remembered that Ramón had told me about it.

A gray-haired woman came out of the house, wiping her hands on her dress and smiling. I knew she was Ramón's mother because they looked alike. She knew me too, for she held out her hand and said good day in Spanish and then spoke my name. She said I looked the way Ramón had described me in the letters he wrote.

Ramón's father was away in the hills, cutting wood for charcoal. He is a maker of charcoal, which he sells in the village. But the rest of the family was there at the table eating when I went in. There were four children, two girls and two boys. The older of the girls was about my age and looked like Ramón, too.

Everyone was eating tortillas, spooning chili out of a big bowl in the middle of the table, rolling it up in the tortillas. Señora Sandoval made me sit down. It was awfully hot chili, the red kind. I didn't eat much of it.

On the wall was a picture of Ramón in a white shirt and his bushy hair combed down. It was a colored picture with a gilt frame and some green and yellow plastic flowers fastened to the bottom.

Ramón's mother saw me looking at it. "My husband took him to Rosalía the day when he was sixteen and they made the picture. It is a good picture of Ramón, I think. Do you think so?"

"Yes," I said. "But it is serious."

"Very serious."

"He laughed much," I said.

"Yes, he laughed. He was born that way. Happy. *Muy contento.*" After the tortillas, Ramón's mother took me along a winding path to the brow of the hill. The children and the three dogs came along.

Under some bushes with bunches of red flowers on them was a cross made of sticks and painted white and hung with a wreath of imitation leaves which were covered with dust. There from the brow of the hill the sea lay far below us. It was deep blue in the hot morning light.

"When Ramón was a boy he liked to come here," Prudencia Sandoval said, "and look at the sea."

"He liked to look at many things," I answered.

"He had a big curiosity. It led him away. Is it good to have a big curiosity?" She looked at me across the bunches of red flowers wilting there in the morning sun. "Is it good? I wonder."

"If he had not gone away from here I would never have known him," I said. "We would never have met."

"He was a good writer of letters. He learned to write in school. He tried to teach the writing to me. Casilda, my older daughter, had always to write for me. Ramón wrote well of you. He used many big words, but they had much beauty, these big words he used about you."

"We were in love," I said. "I came to tell you that I loved your son."

"I see that you speak the truth," Prudencia Sandoval answered. "*Es verdad.*"

"It is the truth," I said.

After a while we went back down the hill, all of us together, and I said goodbye. Ramón's mother hoped that I would go with God, and I wished the same for her. The children wanted to ride in the Blazer, so I piled them in and we rode to the village, the dogs too.

I reached Rosalía at noon. Sybil was back from the beach and asleep under a tree. but she got up and we started down the coast.

July 26

We drove into La Paz late this afternoon. The ferry to Mazatlán had just left, and it won't be back for another week.

It's a pretty town right on the gulf, which is called the Vermilion Sea and the Sea of Cortez and also the Gulf of California. It's on a wide bay, and a spit of land like a snake's tongue runs out to form a cozy little bay within the bay. There's a wharf where small rusty freighters load cotton and unload supplies for the town. Fishing boats are scattered around all over the place.

Since we're to be here a week at least before we take off for Culiacán, I went looking for a job and found one waiting table at a nice hotel called Los Arcos. They pay $2 a day and tips, so I should manage to get a stake before we leave. We'll camp in the car as usual.

Sybil is out now, scouting around for a connection. She has plenty of uppers and downers, but she's used up the heroin she bought from the cook.

July 27

There's a public library down the shore from the hotel that has quite a few books in English. I found a book this morning I've always wanted to read. It's called *The Rime of the Ancient Mariner*. It was written by the same poet who wrote *Kubla Khan*, which I like very much. It's about an old seaman who goes to a festive wedding, where he stops one of the guests and fixes him with his

"glittering eye." The young man wishes to flee
but falls under the mysterious spell of the old
man:

> The Wedding Guest sat on a stone:
> He cannot choose but hear;
> And thus spake on that ancient man,
> The bright-eyed Mariner.

I read the poem clear through, walking along
the shore. There's a sea wall in front of Los Arcos,
and I sat there and read the poem again. Then I
recited parts of it from memory. Small waves were
lapping at the shore, dragging the pebbles back
and forth.

Beyond the bay there's an island that looks
white and ghostly. It's called Espíritu Santo, Holy
Spirit. It is a good place to recite *The Rime of the
Ancient Mariner*.

The only thing was that partway through the
poem my memory let me down. I had to read
that part two times more before I learned it. Maybe it's the uppers and downers I've been using.

July 28

Sybil made a connection—apparently it wasn't
hard. A shoeshine boy was pushing. He had it in
an empty can of shoe polish and passed it over to

her while she was drinking a Coke at La Paloma Café, which is the biggest food emporium in town.

I've made $42 in tips during the three days at Los Arcos, plus $6 in wages.

July 29

Two of the girls were home sick yesterday, with something or other, so I had extra tables to serve. I could hardly drag myself back to the car when I was through, my feet were so swollen. I figured another day like that would find me dead.

It's the first time since I left home that I thought of the easy life I'd had once.

I got to thinking of Ramón and wishing that I was up on the hill among the palm trees beside him. Sybil put on a cassette to cheer me up. Then she used some horse.

"No big deal," she said, passing some to me.

No big deal, I thought.

"If you don't like it, you can quit."

July 30

I felt sick when I got up, but I'd been feeling sick in the morning ever since we arrived in La

Paz. Sybil looked at me suddenly as I was starting off to work.

"You're not pregnant?" she asked.

"No," I answered, since it was the first time I had thought about it.

But before lunch I went to a doctor the hotel manager told me about. The doctor was a young man who has an office in his home. His wife is his nurse. He examined me right away. "Young lady," he said, "you are pregnant."

When I went back to the Blazer after supper was over at Los Arcos and told Sybil, she said, "A little or a lot?" But before we went to bed she got serious.

"How do we have any fun?" she asked me, "if you're running around pregnant? We can't, that's all. Get rid of it. Why do you want to bring a kid into this weirdo world?"

I didn't say anything. She must have thought that I was stunned. I *was* stunned. But not the way she thought. I was so happy, I couldn't talk. Happy that I am going to have Ramón's child. Happy! And scared, too. I'm not sure where I'll go. But it won't be to Culiacán with Sybil. I won't sleep tonight.

August 2

The ferry left this morning for Mazatlán. It's a beautiful ship. (My father taught me when I was only seven not to call a ship a boat and vice versa. A ship is anything over 50 feet long. And it's not an "it" but a "she.") She even has a swimming pool.

Sybil drove the Blazer through the big opening in the stern, put the brakes on, took her bags out, and locked the car. We didn't talk until we were out on the wharf again.

"No hard feelings," Sybil said. "But you're a dope. Anyway you figure, you're a dope. A big one. It's just too much."

The ship's siren gave a blast.

"What are you going to do?" Sybil said.

"I don't know."

"You'll go home."

"No."

"As fast as you can."

"I'll keep working for a while."

"It's not too late. Change your mind. You don't need a bag. There's nothing much in it, anyway."

Another blast from the ship.

"You'll find someone for company," I said. "Maybe on the ship, before you even get to Mazatlán."

Sybil glanced around. There were two young

Mexican officers, all dressed in white and gold braid, standing at the rail of the ship, looking down at us.

"I don't see much except tourists," she said.

"You're not looking very hard."

Sybil didn't look again but she tossed her head. Her hair fanned out over her shoulders.

"Change your mind," she said. "Nobody'll know you're preg. Not for months. Mother went around for five months when she was carrying me before anyone knew."

I didn't say anything. I didn't warn her that she might get herself into big trouble with the false tail pipe she intended to fill with dope as soon as she got to Culiacán. And that I didn't want to be with her if it happened.

"You needn't be scared," she said, reading my thoughts. "If they stop us, I'll say that I just picked you up and you know nothing about nothing."

A great blast from the ship's horn.

"I'll miss you, Sybil."

She smiled and kissed me. But I could tell that already she was thinking of other things. Music. Tropical moons. Boys. Horse. Adventure.

She gave me her handkerchief, with something knotted up in it. "In case you find yourself hanging in the breeze," she said.

I put the handkerchief in my pocketbook. For a moment I didn't want her to go. "You don't know a word of Spanish," I said.

"Sign language is good everywhere," she answered and ran up the gangplank, tossing her head again.

The white ship backed away. We waved and waved and waved.

I have a crummy room with a toilet down the hall in a decrepit house on an alley, but it's only a dollar a night. The light I'm writing by comes from a globe the size of a marble that hangs from a long frayed wire.

There's some of the brown stuff wrapped up in the handkerchief Sybil gave me. I had forgotten it. Or had I? It doesn't matter.

Far off a beginner is playing a guitar. Someone is laughing outside the window. A wind is blowing, and it's so hot I can hardly breathe.

I'm glad Sybil is gone. My feelings about her have changed. In just 24 hours. Since I went to the doctor.

I am happier than I have ever been in my whole life. But still I'm scared. I think I'll use some of the stuff Sybil gave me. Now. I'll sniff it the way she does. Just a little. A little won't hurt, and it may do some good. The King, Sybil calls it.

Yesterday I read the introduction to *The Rime of the Ancient Mariner*. It said that the poet Samuel Taylor Coleridge used opium.

It is cooler now. The King is working, the beginner has magically learned to play the guitar. At least the music sounds sweeter than it did. I no longer feel confused. I'm beginning, at this very moment, to understand what's happened to me. I am happy, happy, happy! What a wonderful thing to have Ramón's child!

I am going to bed now and sleep until noon. Maybe all day!

August 3

The guests at Los Arcos are about half American and half Mexican. They're good tippers. The Mexicans tip more than the Americans.

So far I've taken in $183.55, plus $18 in wages. Not bad. I get my meals free, so I've saved every cent. Mother was always bugging me about spending money. It just shows what I am really like. I owe the rent.

August 4

Today an airmail from Sybil. She wrote before she started north for Culiacán.

She has picked up two hitchhikers, a girl and a young man. She wishes I were there. I'm glad I'm not. While I was serving lunch today, I heard a Mexican telling about all the American women who are locked up in Los Reyes prison in Mexico

City on dope charges. Some of them have been there for five years. I hope Sybil doesn't get locked up.

August 6

Doctor Verdugo gave me a urine test yesterday. This morning he asked me if I was using. I didn't know what to say, so I shook my head and tried to pass it off.

"The test shows quinine," he said. "Have you been drinking quinine water?"

"Yes," I lied. "I drink a bottle or two every day."

Dr. Verdugo didn't believe me, I guess, because he said that pregnant girls shouldn't be using heroin. I agreed with him. He wants me to come in for another test next Thursday. I don't think I'll show up. In fact, I may not be here at all.

I don't know what's turned me off. The work? All that food that I pass out twice a day? I never thought I could ever get tired of huevos rancheros and refried frijoles. But I *am* tired.

And I'm tired of being nice to the customers when I don't feel like it, just because I'm trying for a big tip. Maybe it's the heat. The sun bounces off the bay and the roofs and the cobbled streets as if it were trying to give you an idea of what hell is like.

A lot of people sleep on the beach at night. I think I will, too.

August 7

A million mosquitoes had the same idea, so I got up at midnight and went back to my room, which was steaming.

All day today people were talking about a hurricane. This is the season, said the cook, Señor Gomez. Two years ago, he said, half the town was blown away by a big wind. A hundred-mile-an-hour *huracán* that blew for three days and broke a dam and drowned more than 2000 people.

Now I'm sure that I am going to leave La Paz.

August 8

Sybil phoned just before lunchtime. She's in Culiacán. She didn't say so, but I gathered that she's made a connection or is about to make one. She said that she was not going north to the border after all, since there was trouble at Mexicali and San Luis, but was coming back to Mazatlán and across to La Paz.

I told her that I was thinking about leaving, and

153

she said for me not to split before she got here. She thinks it will be two or three weeks. I told her about Los Reyes prison in Mexico City and all the women who are locked up there. She just laughed.

August 9

I am out of uppers and downers and the King Sybil left. This morning the cook sold me a bottle of cool-looking stuff that some of the girls here at Los Arcos are using. It's called *polvo de angel*, angel dust. It's a zap out.

This afternoon I was out on the wharf watching a ship being loaded. There's a ranch near here where fighting bulls are raised. There were six of them being sent to Mazatlán. Vaqueros herded them onto the wharf and out to the ship. The bulls were very docile. Ynez, a waitress at Los Arcos, was with me—her fiancé is one of the vaqueros—and she said that bulls were docile because the vaqueros gave each of them angel dust.

The bulls looked peaceful, as dreamy as cows, when the men put slings under their bellies and hoisted them aboard.

I felt the same way after I took my first angel dust. But I wish I had a pinch of the brown stuff. I haven't been able to make a connection yet, but I'll keep trying. I have to.

August 10

The tide was out this morning and I walked along the beach in front of Los Arcos. I thought about Samuel Coleridge and how he used opium and wrote beautiful poems. I had *The Rime of the Ancient Mariner* with me. The book is a beaten-up paperback, but the pages have wide margins, and in the margins the editor has comments opposite almost every stanza. They're very helpful in understanding what Coleridge meant. When I first read the poem, it was just fun and exciting when the ship flees south before the howling wind:

And now there came both mist and snow,
And it grew wondrous cold:
And ice, mast-high, came floating by,
As green as emerald.

And then an albatross follows the ship, and when the Ancient Mariner calls, it comes and perches nearby. But the old man kills the friendly bird with his crossbow.

What does the albatross stand for, the editor asks? Is it a sign of God's love? And why does the Mariner kill the bird? Does he turn his back on God? The editor thinks that it is murder. Murder against Nature and Sanctity. He thinks that the

155

old sailor must sooner or later pay for his crime.

The poem means more to me now than it did at first. Did a friendly albatross come at my call? If it came, did I kill it?

The poem upsets me when I really think about it. Yet I want to think about it. I am out of dust. If I could only find some of the Mexican brown, I could think better. I tried the boy who shines shoes. He's going to look around and get in touch.

August 11

I bought a packet this morning, enough to last a week, from the shoeshine boy. It's very expensive, even here in La Paz, just a few miles from where the poppies are grown. It is smoother, more heavenly, than dust. Wow!

August 12

I changed my mind and kept the appointment with Dr. Verdugo. He asked me about the heroin several times. I kept putting him off, trying to make character, because I like him. He's interested in my baby, and he only charges $2 a visit. He wanted to take another urine test. Just a bluff, I figured, but I finally admitted that I had been using.

Dr. Verdugo went over and pushed back the lace curtain. His office is in the parlor of the house. He looked out at the bay shimmering in the sun.

"The fishermen talk about a big wind," I said, thinking to change the subject. "Maybe this week."

Dr. Verdugo didn't answer. He closed the curtains and took off his horn-rimmed glasses and started to polish them with the end of his necktie.

"Do you want to have a healthy baby?" he asked me.

What kind of question was that, I thought. "Of course I do," I said.

"Then you had better get off the dope. If you don't, your baby will be born an addict, the same as you are."

"I am not an addict," I said. He made me mad, standing there polishing his glasses and talking like some sort of a god. "In my whole life I've only used it two or three times."

"Are you using now?"

"Yes."

"Then you are an addict."

"I only use a little."

"With *heroína*," he said and stopped. He put his glasses on and looked through them at the ceiling. "With *el caballo grande* there is no such thing as a little."

His daughter, who is five years old and deformed, was sitting in a playpen in a corner of the room. She was playing with a worn-out doll. I went over and took her hand in mine. She has dainty little hands with perfect fingernails.

"I can quit tomorrow," I said.

"Quit today," Dr. Verdugo said. "If you don't, señorita, you will be the mother of an addicted baby, a little *morfinómano*. Would you like that, señorita?"

August 13

I get a lot of exercise running around the palm-fringed patio at Los Arcos, but I walk to the wharf every morning mostly to watch the fishermen go out. Usually the bay looks like brass, but today it was the color of watered milk. The sailors are still talking about the possibility of a *huracán*.

I'm getting edgy. I haven't used the brown stuff since yesterday morning. I've been thinking about what Dr. Verdugo said. Thinking hard!

August 14

Sybil called this evening just as we were closing the dining room. She said the Arizona border is still hot, so she is definitely going to leave Mexico through La Paz and Tijuana. I told her to be sure and check on the weather before she comes. I told her that everyone was talking about a *huracán*.

I haven't used the Mexican brown for two days now. I feel ratty. Falling-down-not-getting-up ratty. Last night I had a hard time going to sleep. I finally made it by reciting the whole of the *Ancient Mariner* to myself. Most of it, anyway. I don't know exactly why, but it fascinates me.

August 15

Today the sky was no longer scummy-looking. The commercial fishermen went out early and a few of the sport fishermen, too.

One of the sport fishermen is staying at Los Arcos. His name is Spencer Harper. He's been here for three days now and this was the first day he's gone out. He has five fishing poles, and all of them have cases made of pigskin. He must have a dozen reels, also in leather cases. I've been waiting on him at the evening meals.

This afternoon he brought back a whole launch full of fish. All kinds of fish—dolphin, needlefish, roosterfish, bass, yellowtail, red snapper, pompano. One of the big pompano he kept and had the cook broil for his dinner. I brought it in and set it on the table in front of him.

He's a nice-looking man about forty or so, with blue eyes and a baby's pink skin. He drinks a lot, but you wouldn't know it offhand. He looked at the platter with the broiled pompano sitting in the middle, surrounded by parsley and slices of mango and lemon.

"You're a good cook," he said. "Who taught you?"

I went along with his joke. I told him that my mother had taught me. He wanted to know if I was a Mexican.

"On my mother's side," I said.

"Where are you from?" he asked in pretty good Spanish.

I thought of a faraway place I had read about. "Tehuantepec," I said. "I was born there."

"I've heard about Tehuantepec. I hear that it has a lot of pretty girls. Are they all as pretty as you?"

"Some of them," I said.

When Mr. Harper finished his pompano and left, I found two $10 bills under the ashtray.

An American family came tonight. Mother and father and two teen-age girls. One of the girls wandered into the pantry after dinner. She asked me if I could get her some pot. I told her I couldn't and that La Paz marijuana was dangerous. That it was mixed up with other stuff.

August 16

I wonder why *The Rime of the Ancient Mariner* fascinates me so much.

I took the last of the angel dust and went to sleep right away and dreamed that I had something around my neck. At first it was like a snake. Then it was a bird that had large drooping wings and a long neck. Something like a pelican. Then I realized that it was not a pelican, but an albatross. The bird was heavy and kept pulling me down, down, down—into a gray sea.

When I awoke this morning at daylight, I was sweating. I found that I had yanked the bedcover up from the bottom of the bed and had it wound around my throat.

August 18

I stayed awake last night until I took the first of a new supply of *polvo de angel.* I lay and counted the time. I have now been pregnant for eighty-four days. The thought for yesterday was a poem by Robert Frost, but I barely remember it. I keep thinking of the *Ancient Mariner.* I go

over it in my mind at odd times, while I am waiting on guests and walking along the sea wall in
the morning and lying in bed awake.

I think about the old man. How he was
haunted by a guilty conscience and how the ship
was pursued through the sea by avenging furies.
"The charméd water burnt away. A still and awful red."

August 19

It was terrible today. The bay simmered and
seemed ready to catch fire. There was no wind,
not a breath. The palm trees around the hotel were
silent. Except for the scurrying of the rats that
nest there. The rats may know something. I think
that I should leave La Paz. I'll decide tonight,
now.

I have decided. But where will I go? I have
no home. That complicates things.

August 20

Sybil called. She is starting for La Paz next Sunday. She asked me if I had any of the brown stuff
left. When I said no, she said not to worry, she's

bringing plenty, enough for an army. It gave me the shivers just to hear her say it. I didn't tell her I was leaving. I was afraid that she would try to persuade me to change my mind and hang around until she comes.

Sybil scares me. I get along better when she's not around. But still I miss her. I wish I had someone I could really talk to. Somebody straight.

Are there problems in life that just can't be solved?

August 21

Most of the guests have fled. It's the threat of a *huracán*.

But Mr. Harper stays on. He went fishing this morning at daybreak. He wanted me to go with him, but I get seasick just standing on a wharf and watching a boat bob up and down.

I went down after lunch when his launch came in. It was flying a marlin flag and it gave a couple of toots as it rounded the point. When I got there, the marlin was hanging by the tail from a scaffold. Its sword was dripping pale blood and its great eyes had faded in the sun. Mr. Harper stood beside the great fish. He held his rod in one hand and his white, long-billed cap in the other. He smiled as the photographer took his picture. He looked proud, as if he had just climbed Mt. Everest.

He'll be good and drunk at dinner tonight.

Later. He was. He asked me to fly off to Acapulco with him. I told him I get airsick and stay sick for days. And that I was the secretary-treasurer of a club devoted to giving the air back to the birds.

August 22

After lunch today I gave notice at Los Arcos. I've saved $305.11 since I came to Baja. A bus goes north every day at five. I could take a plane, but I need to save money.

It might be better for me to go to San Carlos and be near Ramón's family. Maybe I can stay for a while. Sénora Sandoval has a lot of mouths to feed, but I have money for my board. Considering what the family eats, mostly beans and tortillas, I have enough to stay until I have my baby. If they want me, that is.

August 23

Dr. Verdugo thinks that it's a good idea for me to leave. He says that I should go home. I didn't tell him that I don't have a home to go to.

He told me again to lay off the big H. But he said nothing about poppers, so I'll put in a supply before I leave.

I bought a doll for his little girl. She was happy when I gave it to her and clung to my hand. I hope I don't have a deformed child. A terrible thought!

August 24

One more day and I'll be off. I have my ticket, so there won't be any trouble about a seat. I'll leave word at the hotel for Sybil. I hate to say it, but I pray that she doesn't come. Maybe there'll be a hurricane and the ferry will sink and she can't come. I have horrible thoughts. Can you have horrible thoughts and still be a nice person?

August 25

The Tijuana bus was crowded. Paisanos sitting on the roof, hanging on any way they could. With chickens and washtubs. About a hundred left behind.

The bus driver, who was fat and took up enough room for three people, gave me a ten-second look as I got on. When he came back to collect tickets he gave me another long one.

I wondered if someone in Tijuana had asked him to keep a lookout for Kathleen Winters. How would they describe me? Straight blond hair. Dark brown eyes. Not pretty but has a good figure. Speaks Spanish fluently. Etc.

I was careful not to answer him in Spanish when he asked me where I was going. I pretended I didn't understand. It said plainly on my ticket where I was going, so why did he ask? I was glad to see the last of him when I got off at Santa Rosalía.

I couldn't find a place to sleep, so I am writing this sitting up in the crummy bus station. I popped a red and feel better.

The thought for yesterday was a quotation from Daniel Defoe: "All your discontents spring from want of thankfulness for what you have." Oh, yeah?

August 26

Ramón's family was glad to see me. I got here at noon, just as they sat down to eat. The children saw me walking up the hill and came whooping. Shrieks and hugs and kisses all around.

Cries of "*La Norteamericana! Viva la Norteamericana!*"

It made me feel like one of the Sandovals.

August 27

It's wonderful to be with Ramón's family.

I haven't told his mother that I'm pregnant. I don't think I will, for a while. Not until I know her better. She might be shocked.

Of course, I could say that we were married. We were. We are!

August 30

There's talk here too of a *huracán*. When I went down to the village this morning to buy groceries, the man who owns the store said that tomorrow he was going to board up the window.

The store is named La Tienda Grande but it only has a small counter and a half-dozen shelves. It's a poor store for poor people. The whole village is poor, like the Sandovals.

The family lives on about $2 a day.

Ramón's father makes a little selling charcoal, the older boy finds odd jobs now and then in the village. Most of the money comes from Luz, Casilda's younger sister. She sleeps in a hammock near mine and I hear her slip out in the dark.

After a while I hear pat, pat, pat, as she kneads dough and turns it into tortillas. She makes 50 paper-thin corn tortillas, wraps them in a cloth, and hikes down the trail to the store, where they bring two centavos apiece. Then she comes back up the trail, has her breakfast of tortillas and beans, and walks back down the trail, along with her two brothers, to the one-room school.

She should be tired when she comes home at night, just in time to help with supper, but isn't.

Casilda doesn't do much work around the house. Apparently she made tortillas until she was sixteen, then it became Luz's task. Now that she's finished with school, she sits around and dreams about coming to the United States. Since she knows what happened to Ramón, I'd think it would be the last place in the world she'd want to go.

Whenever she has a chance, she asks me about America. What does it look like? What do Americans eat? How do they dress? How much money can girls make? How much does it cost to live?

Casilda also wants to know about the movies. She has seen one in her life, once when her parents took her to La Paz to be confirmed. She has a pretty, heart-shaped face and gleaming black hair and Ramón's white teeth. I don't encourage her to come to Norteamerica.

September 1

I am doing better here in San Carlos. I've taken only two reds. And I haven't craved the brown stuff. Not really. I guess Dr. Verdugo scared me. I hope it lasts. If Sybil doesn't show up, I'll be all right. Maybe I'll be all right even if she does. Maybe.

September 2

I went up the hill this afternoon. It was late and the sun was going down. I just sat on the hill for a while and thought. What I thought I can't seem to put down in my diary. It's so mixed up. I am beginning to feel that I shouldn't be here. Everywhere I turn I think of Ramón. I see him everywhere.

September 3

Prudencia is the mother of eight children. Four of the children are dead, two of them from smallpox. She is only thirty-three, but she looks twice that age. Gray hair and wrinkles and all the rest. She's not old inside, however. She smiles a lot and likes to tease the two boys. Her husband, Sebastián, whom I haven't seen, spends his time, when he isn't burning wood for charcoal, drinking pulque in San Carlos.

Pulque is cheap, five centavos a glass. I had a glass of it yesterday and it's awful. If the big H looked as bad as pulque does, I'd have no problem.

September 6

The Vermilion Sea is not far away. You can hear it sometimes. From the hill where Ramón's buried you can almost see it stretching eastward to the mainland, where Sybil is.

Yesterday afternoon flocks of sea gulls came from the sea and flew over the house, making a great racket. Then they flew back toward the sea. They seemed to be confused. Toward sunset the sky turned yellow and then dark clouds came in from the south. Low across the sea.

At supper I asked Prudencia if she thought a storm was coming.

She shrugged her shoulders. *"Es posible,"* she said.

I think that is her philosophy — It is possible. A *huracán*. Sudden death. Smallpox. Anything is possible.

"If the wind comes," she said, "we will hide. There is a cave nearby at the bottom of the hill, and we will go there and hide until the wind leaves."

September 9

The hurricane struck two days ago, early in the morning. The night before, while we were eating supper, the first warning came over Casilda's pink radio. She bought the radio with some of the money Ramón sent home, and she carries it around with her wherever she goes and takes it to bed with her at night.

The warning started in the afternoon. The Mexicans have copied the Norteamericanos and give the wild winds the names of girls. This one is called Rosa María. After supper, while the news was coming in, Prudencia dug a hole and buried a basket of tortillas. Then she packed a lot more of them and we all trooped down the hill, sat by the entrance to the cave, and watched the sky dim over and the stars disappear.

Everyone was asleep except me when the big wind came.

Just before daylight I heard it rustling in the palm trees. Softly, at first. Then it banged the fronds around as though they were made of metal. I shook Prudencia awake, she awakened the rest,

171

and we all ran far back into the cave, as far as we could go, which was about 20 steps, and crouched there in the darkness.

Casilda's radio fell silent. You couldn't hear the palm trees clashing any longer. There was a great roar now, like freight trains running across the sky. Prudencia tried to light a candle but the draft put it out.

Dawn broke with a yellow light over everything. We didn't dare go near the mouth of the cave. We could see brush and shreds of trees flashing past. The roar kept up. All that morning, we crouched in the yellow darkness.

Prudencia said, "When I was big with Ramón and could scarcely walk there was another *huracán*. That was the first time it came. We stayed here in the cave for three days. It was terrible when we went out. There was nothing left of our house, nothing except the hard dirt floor. But we, the two of us, were safe."

She tried again to light a candle. Kneeling there in the yellow shadows, she put a hand over her heart. "It is good to have the cave," she said, "but in it you cannot hide from everything."

We looked at each other. Her face was like stone.

"Not from all things," I said.

Casilda held the silent radio in her lap as if it were a sick child. "In Norteamerica do you have the big wind?" she asked me.

"Yes," I said, "and other things besides the big wind."

By noon the wind had died down somewhat. Prudencia went to the mouth of the cave and looked out. We all gathered around her. Tops of trees lay scattered about. The wind came in gasps now, like a great animal dying. Casilda's pink radio sputtered, came on, and went off. We couldn't pick up any of the news from La Paz. The wind was still strong, but blowing in gusts. We went back in the cave and waited.

September 10

Morning dawned quietly. Not a sound anywhere except some quail calling in the brush.

We went up the trail. The house was gone. No sign of it anywhere. The palm trees stood, but their branches were stripped away, down to the bare trunks.

"It is like the first time," Prudencia said. "The same."

The boys were excited. They began to run around looking for things that had belonged to them.

Casilda's pink radio had come on and we got the first news we'd had for days. It trickled in from La Paz, mixed with music. Rosa María had struck an uninhabited part of the countryside and

173

was blowing itself out over the mainland, beyond the Sea of Cortez. Two fishing boats had foundered, but the crews were safe.

Prudencia said, "We will have to sleep on the ground tonight. But tomorrow, if La Tienda Grande has not blown away, we have the hammocks."

At dusk we built a fire and heated the tortillas that Prudencia had buried. The pink radio got more news from Santa Rosalía. For one thing, the Mazatlán–La Paz ferry will resume its regular schedule on Wednesday, the 15th.

My prayers were not answered. I am an awful person. Really. I am glad I still have a few poppers on hand.

September 15

Friends have come in from the hills during the last two days, from places where the wind did not strike, bringing peeled poles and thatch for a roof.

We all helped to put up a *ramada*. The weather, Prudencia thinks, will be fair from now on, clear through the winter, so nothing more is needed than this lean-to.

Sebastián showed up from somewhere with a bundle of secondhand clothes, mostly for the boys. He and two men built an oven out of stones, and for supper we had frijoles and a rabbit that a friend had brought in.

Sebastián left this afternoon with his burro. He seems glad to come and glad to go. He's friendly enough but I don't know whether he likes me or not. Probably not. Why should he?

I'm getting nervous about being here. I wonder if I shouldn't be moving on. Not home. But somewhere.

September 17

The children went off to school this morning.

Luz was up at her regular time and made a batch of tortillas from flour I'd bought at the store, which managed to survive the hurricane. Then she went off with the boys down the trail to San Carlos and school.

School starts this week at Point Loma.

With everything that's happened, I'd feel funny sitting in a classroom. The pregnant Miss Kathleen Winters listens to Miss Mary Lou Bartlett expounding on the virtues of good citizenship.

All that seems long ago. In another world.

I feel at home here. Prudencia treats me like a daughter. Her girls are sweet.

If it's the last thing I do, I'll keep Casilda from running off to the U.S.

September 18

Yesterday Luz brought some homework from school. Math, which doesn't come easy, but I helped her a little. Oddly, I picked up a few things myself. She's studying English, too, and I helped her with that. The two boys are shy when they're around me.

The days are very hot. But living in a *ramada*, sleeping in a hammock, is fun. Like camping out, sort of.

September 21

Now that all the reports are in, it appears that a lot of families near the sea suffered from the hurricane. The government is thinking about sending supplies and things, but nothing has arrived yet. In the meantime, buzzards are congregating.

September 22

This morning a red helicopter flew over. At first I thought it was Sybil. Just like her, I thought, to hire a helicopter and horse around, just for kicks. But it flew up and down the ridge for about an hour. Finally it flew so low I could see the pilot and a man with him.

We didn't know until Luz came home from school what the two men were doing. Her teacher said that they had been sent out by the Mexican government to search for fields of illegal crops.

Apparently there are thousands of small farms scattered around in the wild parts of the country where farmers are cultivating opium and marijuana plants.

While we were eating breakfast—a bowl of frijoles and two tortillas apiece—we heard voices on the trail. It was Sybil and her friends, a redhaired girl about my age, and a young man with a white scar on his chin.

"Hey, baby!" she hollered. "What's happening?"

As we wrapped our arms around each other, I felt cold all over. She was high. Floating.

She glanced around at the family. At the meager bowls of frijoles. The hammocks strung between the trees. She said she had to go to the toilet, and I pointed to some bushes a couple of hundred feet away. She made a face and didn't go.

She and her girl friend, Tamara, wouldn't eat, but the thin young man ate all the frijoles and all the tortillas that were left.

Sybil and her friends hung around for a while and then trooped off down the trail, the young man playing "El Rancho Grande" on his guitar.

Sybil made me promise to come down to San Carlos and have lunch with them. I didn't want to go but there wasn't any way out.

I knew what would happen. I no sooner got there and climbed into the Blazer, which was parked in a little palm grove on one side of the plaza, than Sybil asked me what I'd been using.

"Reds," I told her.

"Kid stuff," she said and handed me a dollar bill folded up in the shape of a funnel. In it was a snort of brown horse. "Try this. You need it."

I took the heroin and just held it in my lap.

Sybil said, "We're taking off in the morning. You'd better pack up tonight so you'll be here early. I want to make the desert before it gets hot."

My hands began to sweat. "I'm going to stay for a while," I said. "Another two weeks, maybe."

Sybil looked at me with her mouth open. She looked at me for a long time. "You must be kidding," she said. "You're out of your skull."

"I like the family," I said. "I like San Carlos."

"You've got to be romancing."

"I'm not."

"You like to eat frijoles?"

"Yes."

"And tortillas?"

"Yes."

"You like them every meal?"

I didn't answer.

"You like to squat in the bushes?"

I still didn't answer. I had made up my mind to leave, but not for these reasons. I was silent.

Sybil reached out and gave my hand a nudge. "Loosen up. Take a snort. It's perfection. Uncut."

The thin young man quit banging on the guitar long enough to say, "Perfection, brother Man; utterly perfection."

"No fooling," Sybil said. "Pull yourself together. You can't stay around here and live like a peon. How soon is the baby?"

"Not tomorrow."

"It'll be a weakling, you living on beans and stuff like that. In a month it will be dead, of smallpox or something. Half the Mexican kids die from one thing or another before they're two years old. Typhoid or smallpox or amoebic dysentery—you name it, they've got it."

She paused and nudged my hand again. A thought came to her. "Are you hanging around here on account of Ramón? It isn't healthy, hanging around."

"Let's split now," the red-haired girl said to the guitar player. "This place gives me the creeps."

I clung to to the dollar bill folded into a cornucopia that held a snort of the stuff that looked like brown sugar. It burned in my hand. Sybil was watching me.

"Have a snort and snap out of it," she said.

"I'm off," I said.

"You were never on," she answered. "Really."

While Sybil was watching me, I thought about

Dr. Verdugo's warning. I heard his words clearly: "You had better get off the dope. If you don't, your baby will be born an addict. . . ." I got up and put the cornucopia on the shelf and sat down again.

"I don't want it," I said. "I don't need it."

September 23

I went down to the store and bought $36.45 worth of flour and frijoles. Enough food to last for three months. And two cartons of orange crush for the children. I wish I could do more.

There's not much I can do. I know that I'll never be at home here. Everyone is friendly, but the truth is, I feel like a visitor. A curiosity. The girl from Los Estados Unidos. Ramón's sweetheart. It's a feeling I'm getting more and more.

Now and then the feeling is more than that. It's a sharp, hurtful pain under my breastbone.

Ramón is dead. He lies in a grave on the hill. But still he lives in my heart and in my body, and I can take him with me. He will go wherever I go.

I haven't much time to pack, luckily. I'll do it in the morning.

September 25

We've been on the road now for almost two days, bound for Tijuana and the States—Sybil and Tamara and me, Freddie and his guitar.

It was hard leaving. When I was able to put aside the stuff Sybil carefully fixed for me—all the time watching every breath I took, wanting me to use it—right then I decided to leave. Right then I knew that she couldn't tempt me anymore. I could stand up to her.

I felt like the Ancient Mariner when he was freed from the albatross.

All the family cried, even the two boys, who seldom spoke to me. Prudencia most of all because, I guess, she has the most to cry about. Casilda wailed when she couldn't go along. If I ever have a home, I'll ask the family to visit me. And I am going to send Prudencia some money as soon as I find a job, which I'll need to do when I get to the States.

$226 left.

I didn't go up on the hill where Ramón is buried. It was too much.

September 26

Sybil has heroin stashed away in the phony tail pipe. She's going to keep half of it and sell the rest.

I worry. What if we get stopped by the Mexican *federales,* or customs find it when we cross the border? I would be liable, too, I guess, though I didn't buy it and I don't own the car or anything.

Sybil doesn't worry so I won't either.

I've used the last of my reds.

September 27

We've all been visited by Montezuma's revenge. I hope it isn't amoebic, which lasts for several years or until you die.

September 28

Hot and sticky.

Freddie's guitar is changing shape in the heat. It's getting to look like a pretzel, and strange notes come out of it. I like Freddie. Too bad he's hooked on horse. Tamara is kooky but I like her, too. Sybil has a taste for kooks. I guess that's why she likes me.

September 30

We passed the last of the Mexican checkpoints without any trouble, the one at Estero. I jumped out and talked Spanish to the same young man we'd met before and he waved us on with a smile. Sybil took the guitar away from Freddie and locked it up before we got there. She should keep it locked up until we cross the border. We look enough like weirdos without the guitar.

We plan to cross the border tonight, about eleven, when the jai alai crowds are leaving.

October 7

In the hospital.

Seven days have gone and I haven't written a single line in my diary.

What a horrible week!

How can so many horrible things happen in one week?

But I guess I'm lucky just to be alive. I guess.

I am not sure. Maybe it would be better if I were dead. I wish I were.

I have lost my baby. The nurse told me today. She sat down on the bed and held my hand and told me.

October 8

I felt better today. Not much, but a little. At this rate it will take me a year to get myself together. Maybe the rest of my life.

October 9

My temperature was normal today, the nurse said. The way I feel, I doubt that she's right. I think she's just trying to buck me up. Why bother?

October 10

Sun today for a change. The curtains were pulled back, and I could see the islands in the sea. The Coronados. They're named after the famous explorer. He never got this far north, but his name did somehow.

I have been asking about Sybil for the last three days. The nurse's answer has been that everyone was all right. But today, after she took my temperature and found that it was normal—two days in a row—she told me that Sybil is dead, that she died on the way to the hospital. That everyone in the car that night is dead, except me. God in heaven, why me? Why was I spared? Oh, God!

October 11

This is the first day that I haven't had a headache. My memory's coming back. I'm beginning to remember things. But maybe it would be better if I didn't.

Sybil wanted to go to the Gatito Café, but I had bad vibes about the place, mostly about my mother. Seeing her standing there and the colored lights flashing and her shouting my name.

We went to the Paloma instead. We stayed there until jai alai was over and the crowd began to head north. We got into the line of cars heading for San Diego.

As we stopped for a red light, two sailors came running out and asked if they could grab a hitch across the border. Sybil told them to pile in. To me she said, "They're good decoys. Customs never bother the gobs."

We inched along, pulled up at the station, held

our breaths until the officer waved us on. The sailors jumped out as soon as we crossed the line and disappeared. I don't know what they were up to. No good, I'm sure.

While we were stopped, Sybil unlocked Freddie's guitar and told him to play and quit talking. She had been popping reds all the time we were in Tijuana, so she was high when we pulled away from the border. Driving crazy-like. As if there weren't any other cars on the road. She scared me, but I didn't say anything. Freddie got scared too and asked her if she wanted him to drive and she said if he didn't like it to get out and walk.

It was about this time, about two minutes later, that everything happened.

Sybil was going about sixty, passing a truck and trailer, when she lurched over and gave the truck a broadside bump. The car lifted on two wheels, came down, swerved, and hit a railing. Then skidded and turned over.

I remember banging my head on the windshield, seeing stars, hanging on to a broken door, feeling the car turn over on its back, like a bug, with its wheels in the air. That's all. No screams. No pain. Afterward, a big blank.

October 12

This morning, when the nurse brought my breakfast, she told me that there was a man in the hallway who wished to see me.

"He's been here before," she said. "Twice. A couple of hours after you were admitted and again two days ago."

"He must be an insurance man," I said.

"No, he's from the police department. He showed me his badge. I've held him off for days. I can't any longer."

His name was Larson. A smiling young man and full of apologies, but he handed me a warrant and said that I was under arrest for possession.

"Possession of what?"

"Drugs," he said. He smiled, apologized for the intrusion, and said he would be back at two o'clock that afternoon.

As soon as he left, the nurse wanted to know if I was guilty. Not right out, but she asked a lot of questions. I finally told her the whole story, the principal part being that Sybil must have put heroin in my pocketbook the night we were in Tijuana. Anyway, there was some of the stuff lying around, I guess.

The rest of the morning I thought about splitting, just walking out when the nurse wasn't around.

At noon I combed my hair and used the lipstick the nurse gave me. After she brought in my lunch tray and left, I went over to the door and glanced out. But at the end of the corridor, reading a newspaper, or pretending to, was the tall young man, Detective Larson.

October 13

I am writing this in Cell 17, Block A, San Diego City Jail. But tomorrow I'll be out on bail. Mrs. Peterson, the nurse, is going to put up for me. $1500. And I've known her for only a short time. Would I do the same for her, a stranger? The answer is no. But I hope I can do something for her someday. She's a real friend.

The accident was reported by all the papers, but not Sybil's name or mine. It will take them a long time to straighten this out. With our fake names and all.

My roommate, or strictly speaking, my cellmate, is a girl by the name of Bonnie. I don't know her last name. She's from Texas somewhere and is in for possession, the same as I am. She says it's a bum rap, that she isn't guilty. But she's already planning to do some holding when she gets free.

If I ever get out of here I'll never come back, believe me.

This is another world. I don't like it. Think of being in a hole like this for three or four years! I'd rather be dead. There's a woman screaming down the corridor somewhere. I feel like screaming myself.

October 14

There was some kind of a foul-up and I didn't get out on bail this morning. One more day of this and I'll be climbing the walls.

I'm curious about the dope that Sybil stashed away in the tail pipe. Not that I need it, exactly, but if I ever do there's a lot of it. Enough for a lifetime. I feel terrible. I could use some now.

October 15

I am free on bail and my trial isn't coming up until the 29th. I should be able to locate Sybil's Blazer by that time. I hope.

October 16

I have a room at the YWCA. It seems like a good idea, if the judge asks me where I am living.

Roundabout, through the police matron, I found that the car was totaled and sits in a wrecking yard in Chula Vista. I can take a bus down here, but I can't come back on the bus with a tail pipe under my arm. I hope somebody hasn't bought it already. But how do I know that the dope wasn't scattered all over the street when the car was turned upside down and wrecked?

I'll figure out a plan by tomorrow.

October 17

The matron gave me my money back when I left, so I took $26 of the $219 and hired a car.

I told the proprietor of the wrecking yard that I wanted a pipe for a '77 Chevy Blazer. There must have been a million cars in the wrecking yard but he had no trouble locating the Blazer. It was a mess. Looked as if it had fallen off a ten-story building. How did I ever get out alive?

The pipe wasn't too good. In fact, the proprietor wasn't keen on selling it to me, it was so banged up. But I told him my brother was a mechanic and could straighten it out like new. He charged me five bucks.

I drove down to the beach just below the Coronado Hotel, parked the car near an abandoned shack, and dragged the pipe out. It was too tough to straighten out, so I went back to town, bought a plumber's snake, went down to the beach again, and wrestled for most of an hour, taking my time and being careful.

The dope was wrapped in a cloth that had been soaked in wax. It was about an inch and a half in diameter and a foot long. I tossed the tail pipe in some bushes, opened the package, and shook out a snort.

Dr. Verdugo, I kept my word. As long as it made a difference.

I'll bet this is the first horse ever hidden under a mattress in a YWCA.

I don't feel so hot right at the moment, but I'm going to like this stuff real well. I'll take it easy at first, however.

October 20

Today was the second snort I've taken. It dusted me out.

But now, here in my room, I am coming down. I keeping thinking of Sybil and Tamara and

191

Freddie. Freddie, who only wanted to play his guitar and sing. And little pansy-faced Tamara, who wanted to be a dancer and tried hard to speak good English. And poor Sybil. And poor little Kathleen.

I keep thinking of a quotation that was in my diary back in August. It was by William Shakespeare:

> Golden lads and girls all must
> As chimney sweepers, come to dust.

October 22

I bought a San Diego *Union* today and looked up the personals, thinking there might be something for me. There was. Just like back in July: "Kathleen, please come home!" Same words. Same exclamation point. Everything. Mother must have a year's rate.

October 25

I am still taking the horse at a slow trot. I don't want to go at a gallop. I don't want to get hooked on this stuff.

October 27

I went to the courthouse and talked to one of the clerks, who asked me if I had a lawyer. I told her that I didn't want a lawyer. She said that the court would appoint a lawyer to represent me, but I told her that I wanted to tell my story just the way it happened. She warned me that I was charged with a felony and that I could very well end up in jail for a couple of years, so I have a lawyer.

October 28

I didn't use horse today.

October 29

I was too excited to sleep, so I took a couple of downers in the middle of the night. At ten this morning I was in Judge Cranston's courtroom. The courtroom was crowded and my case didn't come up for a long time. I sat and got cold and hot and cold again.

Judge Cranston had white, bushy eyebrows and little tufts of white hair sticking out of his ears. He seemed to be dozing. At least his eyes were closed when my case was called, but when I went up to the bench and held up my right hand and swore to tell the truth and nothing but the truth, his eyes slowly opened. They were pale blue and unfriendly.

Then my charge was read by the clerk, and the judge asked me if I was guilty or not guilty. When I said I was not guilty, he nodded his head as if he had heard the words before.

I had trouble with my voice when my lawyer put me on the stand. It sounded funny and weak, and my mouth got dry, but I managed to squeeze my story out.

It was a true story, but it sounded fishy, even to me, as I told it from the very beginning from the time Sybil made the cornucopia down in San Carlos to the night of the accident. And what I remembered of the accident itself.

I didn't mention my baby.

The judge stopped me only once. I was describing Freddie and Tamara, and he said to get on with my story, he wasn't interested in either one of them. When I finished he sat for a while looking around the courtroom. He shuffled some papers, spoke under his breath to the clerk. Then he looked at me and said he believed most of my story and that because of my age he didn't want to send me to prison. Then he pronounced sentence.

Tomorrow at ten o'clock I am to report to Tranquillity House, which is located in San Diego. It's a place for young dope addicts they don't want to send to jail, I learned from the matron, and for young users who have been in jail and are now trying to go clean.

That's all I know about Tranquillity House, except that it's part of Crash, Inc.—Community Resources and Self-Help, an organization. It can't be any worse than Cell 17, Block A.

October 30

I spent most of the evening trying to figure out where to hide my package of horse.

I thought of leaving it in a locker at the Greyhound Bus station. But there's probably a time limit on occupancy, and no telling when I might be able to get back. I could lose it.

I'm not going to use the dope, ever, now that I am out of jail, but it's worth at least $10,000, from what Sybil told me. Maybe twice or three times if it's cut. I have no intention of selling it on the street, but somehow I might make a sale to a hospital or a charity or something like that.

I finally decided to hide it down on the beach where I left the tail pipe. Tomorrow morning I'll dig a deep hole, up high on the beach away from the tide, and wrap the package in layers of heavy paper. I'll drive three small stakes about thirty feet apart and the hole will be in the center of the triangle. Then I'll smooth out the sand so no one will find my footprints. When that's done I'll buy a newspaper and see if there's anything about the trial in it. I hope not. It's good that I have a phony I.D. That my name is Hilary Coleridge.

November 3

I buried the dope today.

November 5

Tranquillity House is in an old section of the city. It's a two-story house painted white, just like all the other houses on the street. With some ragged palm trees out front and a devilgrass lawn that's turning brown.

There are three counselors officially associated with the house: Mary Lou Crawford, Jane Forsythe, and Jeb Whitman. They don't live there, but come and go at odd times. There are ten of us in the house now, counting myself. We call ourselves the Family.

The three counselors oversee the house, but the Family runs it according to the rules, all set down in black and white on the bulletin board, which is in the hallway as you enter and can't miss. The rules are simple: No sex. Any kind, any time. No drugs, no alcohol, no violence. No threats of violence. For infractions you receive the old boot. Not into the street. But into jail, where you would have been all the time if the court hadn't been nice and sent you here to Tranquillity House.

November 8

Every week or two the Family has a meeting. It's called a Dutch Rub, for some reason. The idea is to sit a brother or sister down and give him or her a good working-over. The ten members in the house can write down their gripes on slips of paper and deposit them in a box. When the box is full, the Foreman calls a meeting.

My Dutch Rub came this morning.

It was held in the basement, which is fixed up like a playroom with three benches, a couple of chairs, some weight-lifting equipment, and an old pool table with a tilt to the left, which someone has donated and no one has bothered to fix.

Six members of the Family were sitting around when I got there, and one of the counselors, Jane Forsythe. I didn't close the door when I walked in, and someone invited me to do so. "Were you raised in a barn?" A bad start.

Harvey Holden is the Foreman. A new Foreman is elected every month. Harvey is about twenty with mild blue eyes and a way of talking that sounds more like a bark than talk. He's in Tranquillity House for pushing.

Two months is the end of the line. After that, if your record is clean, you go out on probation. If it isn't clean, then you go to jail. You either make it in two months, or you don't. It's up to you.

The Foreman took a slip out of the box. It had Joy Thompson's name on it.

Joy is my roommate. She's a big-boned farm girl from Texas somewhere. We have single beds at opposite sides of a room on the second floor, and we share a dresser that has six drawers.

Joy is in for possession and shoplifting.

The member who's written the slip is responsible for it and must speak up.

The Foreman handed the slip to Joy, who read it over to herself. There hadn't been any words between us, so I was very surprised to hear her start running her feelings about me. She talks slowly and slurs her words, but the gist of what I heard was that I hadn't tuned in and I wasn't even trying to.

Joy went on, "We have the same room together but she never speaks. She's all wrapped up in herself."

It's a curious feeling to hear something about yourself from a stranger, something you never thought of, that doesn't sound true but possibly could be.

I was so surprised I just sat there and looked dumb. Daisy Frazer, who was once blond, then red, and is now a little of both, spoke up and said she didn't agree with Joy.

Joy said nothing more, and the Foreman gave a slip to Bruce Kinkaid.

Bruce had some compliments for me, and I got to thinking that he had a crush. Then he said that I acted as if I were carrying a trunk on my back and the trunk was full of bad vibes.

I guess Bruce is right. I do need to lighten the load. I guess it rubs off on other people.

I gave Bruce a smile just to prove that I could smile, and then the Foreman passed Bette the slip she'd written and she took up the cudgel.

She said that I hadn't tried to relate to anyone in the House, which is true. I've been busy relating to myself, trying to put the pieces back together. Should you put yourself together before you try to relate? Or should it be the other way around?

Daisy Frazer was into drugs heavy and wrote checks all over the place to pay for them. She's from New York State via Hollywood via Tijuana. She has a million tiny freckles and is so ugly she's cute. She got on me too about being cold and distant.

That was the last "rub." When I left, they called in another member.

I was glad to leave. I have no plans for writing a slip against anyone. I have enough to do just taking care of myself. The counselor, Jane Forsythe, didn't open her trap the whole session. She's smart.

November 9

Today was my turn to help in the kitchen. I never cared for kitchen work at home, but I don't mind it here. While I was washing dishes, I kept thinking about the horse stashed away on the beach. I've got to stop thinking about it.

November 10

The counselors encourage you to find a part-time job. They say that it's helpful to have contact with the outside world and to have money in your pocket. Also it will help me, I hope, to get my mind in order. For one thing, I'll quit thinking about the stuff I've got stashed away. I hope.

The trouble with getting a job is that I don't have any skills. I can't type or run a machine of any kind or help in a laboratory. I can't do anything except sell clothes and wait table. I am a dummy. A real dummy. The world's biggest.

November 13

The "Kathleen, please come home" item is still running in the *Union*.

I can't see myself back in my old room, getting ready to go to work or to school or anywhere. But maybe I should write Mother a letter and tell her to save her money, that I am not coming home. I'm not angry with her any longer, I just don't have any feelings.

Perhaps what Joy and Daisy said about me not relating, being cold, is true.

The albatross is off my neck now, but I am still confused and uncertain about things. I wonder if I will ever be able to put my life together again.

November 14

I've found a job at Taco Kitchen, working fifteen hours a week at the minimum wage, plus tips. Funny, I'll work for peanuts and all the time there's that stash down on the beach. And with plenty. Ten thousand. Twenty thousand. Maybe more. Real funny!

Today I wrote a letter to Prudencia. She can't read, but Casilda can read it to her. I sent her a money order for $15 and asked her to buy something for herself, which she won't do.

Today is the first day the "Kathleen, please come home" item hasn't run in the newspaper. I don't know why, but I have an odd feeling about it. I guess Mother has given up on me. Perhaps I should call her and let her know that I'm still alive. Half alive, anyway.

The last week, since the Dutch Rub when Joy complained about me, how I treated her as if she wasn't around, things have been worse between us.

This morning I made an effort to break the ice. I usually take my shower first, but this morning I asked her if she wanted to take hers first. She hesitated, mumbled something or other, but went into the bathroom. There wasn't much hot water and she used it all.

When my turn came, the water turned cold just

as I had soap all over my chest. I yelled bloody murder and when I got out I told her that I thought she was very inconsiderate.

"I've always saved hot water for you," I said. "You could do the same for me, couldn't you?"

Joy didn't say anything for a moment. Then she began to cry. She flung herself on the bed and cried all the time I was getting dressed.

I was late already, being on early-morning kitchen duty, but for some reason I stopped as I was going out the door and went back and put a hand on her shoulder. She was still sobbing.

"I'm sorry," I said. "I didn't mean to hurt your feelings. You can use all the hot water you want. I'll take my shower later in the day. I once went a whole week without a shower."

She quit sobbing and glanced up at me from swollen eyes. I guess she was trying to make out whether I meant what I'd said.

"I mean it," I told her. "Tomorrow I'll take my shower when I go to bed."

"It isn't that," Joy said.

She was silent again.

"What's wrong?" I asked.

"Nothing."

I kept at her. "What's bugging you?"

After a while she quit crying and began to talk. She must have talked for all of ten minutes without stopping.

It turns out that it's not me that's been giving her the trouble. It's being off dope. She hasn't used since she's been here, but now it's gotten to her. She wants to split. She begged me to go with her.

"Where?" I asked.

"Anywhere," she said.

"We don't have a car. We'd have to hitch. The cops would have us inside of twenty-four hours."

"We don't need to leave town. We can hide somewhere. Hole up in a room somewhere."

"Without money?" I didn't let on that I had a little. "How do we pay the rent? How do we eat? How do we buy pills or pot or horse without money?"

She kept on and on, trying to make sense. Finally I persuaded her to cool it until tomorrow. I told her I would think it over and maybe figure out something.

November 17

I thought about it last night after I went to bed.

I don't want to say anything to the counselors, but maybe I should. They've had a lot of experience with members splitting. One of the girls took off two weeks ago. I'm sleeping in her bed. But if I do tell them about Joy, they might remand her. Just for her own good. Maybe I should talk to Harvey Holden, the Foreman, and get his advice.

Would I be snitching? I don't think she'll go it alone.

This evening just before supper I had a chance to talk to Joy. I made her promise not to do anything without me.

I don't know how I got myself into this, making myself responsible for someone else. I have enough to do trying to keep Kathleen Winters right side up. Or should I say Hilary Coleridge? Which is my name here.

November 18

I didn't have much to offer Joy this morning when we were getting dressed.

She has a good figure. Like an ancient goddess. But she's clumsy and her face is heavy. It's more suited to a boy than a girl. She has a sister who, she says, is small and pretty. I guess this always made Joy feel clumsier and uglier than she really is.

I asked her if she'd work if I found her a job, and she said maybe. She's ready to climb the wall. I wouldn't be surprised if she leaves without me.

November 19

Joy's asleep on the other side of the room. She's gotten through another day. I still haven't made up my mind about talking to the Foreman or to one of the counselors. She is twisting and turning and muttering in her sleep.

I don't feel so hot myself. I can't get the stash off my mind. Last night I even dreamed about it.

November 20

This morning I told Joy that she should go to one of the counselors, perhaps Jane Forsythe, who is very smart. She doesn't want to. Maybe I should see a counselor, too. I feel something horrible building up in me.

November 21

Joy wasn't so ratty today, but I can't say the same for myself. I've gotten to be a human yo-

yo. One day up. One day down. I need something to space me out.

I'm getting tired of this place. Everybody has a big problem. Joy's problem has almost got me down. I've tried to help her and all I've done is to make things worse for both of us. At least it seems that way.

November 22

I've decided to dig up the stash.

November 24

Joy was real daffy this morning when she came to. Talking wild, making threats that she's going to kill herself, etc. I was afraid to leave her alone when I went to work, so I took her along. It seemed to quiet her down, just being away from the place. I should talk to Jane Forsythe.

November 26

Nothing. Except that it rained hard this afternoon and I'm worrying about the packet. If it got wet. Also, heavy tides have been running all week. I'll have to find a new place to hide it.

November 28

Thanksgiving. The Family demolished a 25-pound turkey, donated by generous citizens of the community. Along with five pies, two mince and three pumpkin. I thought about last year at this time and it made me sad. I wonder where I'll be next Thanksgiving? I hope I'll have more to be thankful for than I do now.

November 29

Joy was a big handful this morning. The Thanksgiving festivities might have upset her, because some time in the night she got to thinking about her mother and father. When I woke up she was sobbing her heart out. I went over and sat on the side of the bed and held her hand until she calmed down.

After a while Joy started talking about how her sister had gotten the best of everything and most of the love and how she got fed up and left home early in the morning without leaving a note, just as I did, and walked to the highway, which was four miles from the farm, and hitched a ride with people who were going to Dallas.

She was going to find someone to love, someone who loved her, she said.

"I hung around there for a week or so, until my money ran low—I only had seventy-six dollars I'd saved up babysitting—then I hitched a ride west as far as Socorro. That's in New Mexico. Socorro means 'help' in English. I stayed there a month. It's an old Spanish town. Everyone was friendly and I got a job in a carwash place. There was a lot of pot around so I got to using. Not much. Not on the job. But afterward sometimes, when the kids were sitting around after work. I stayed in Socorro almost a month, saved up more than two hundred dollars, and struck out for the coast. I'd heard about Hollywood, so that's where I headed."

Joy stopped suddenly. She cried for a while and then she rubbed her eyes with the back of her hand and began again.

"It was outside of Welton—that's in Arizona—a farm town with a lot of orange trees around and vineyards. I was standing at the side of the road near an onramp. This car came along going fast, going my direction. They went past a ways. Then they backed up and stopped. The driver asked me if I wanted a lift. I said yes and climbed in. There were four people in the car, two men and two girls, all of them older than me but not by much. I got in the back next to one of the girls.

"They'd been drinking, passing a bottle that was

about half full, and when I got settled they offered me a drink. I said I didn't drink and they said they were glad to meet someone who didn't.

"There was a lot of laughing until the bottle was finished, then everyone was quiet. It was close to sunset and the country was very pretty with a gold light over everything, even over us. Ahead, off to our right, stood this clump of cottonwood trees and a big pond. The driver said something to the girl next to him, which she didn't like, I guess, because she turned her shoulder and stared out the window.

"The driver's name was Mort. He had a big neck, like football players have, and red hair that came down over his collar, and sideburns that slanted forward and ended in a sharp point. I had a good look at him, as I sat there not two feet away, and I would know him if I ever saw him again.

"When we got near the pond and the clump of cottonwoods, Mort turned down this dirt road that angled off the highway and parked beside the pond. Everyone piled out, and Tony, the other fellow, opened the trunk and pulled out another bottle of whiskey and a bag of McDonald's hamburgers. I took one of the hamburgers and walked down through the cottonwoods to the edge of the pond. Two ducks that were floating on the water flew away as I came through the trees.

"I was standing there, munching away and watching the light change across the water, when

Mort strolled out of the trees. He didn't say anything to me. He just reached out and took my half-eaten hamburger and tossed it in the pond. Then he told me to lie down in the grass. I didn't know what he meant. He told me again to lie down and I saw that he had a knife in his hand.

"He must have known that I was going to scream because he held the knife at me and said if I did he would cut my throat. The others were close by. I could hear them joking. He gave me a push and I fell down. He held the knife at my throat all the time.

"When I got up the other man was standing over me. He said, 'Why don't you throw her in the pond, Mort?' Mort said it wasn't such a good idea. While they were arguing, I got up and ran. I screamed and ran back through the cottonwoods toward the highway, where some trucks were passing. When I came to where the girls were, one of them threw a rock at me. I ran to the highway and kept running until a man in a car picked me up. He was going east, the wrong way, but I rode with him back to Welton."

Joy quit talking. She lay there, rigid and white, for a long time.

November 30

I didn't want Joy Thompson along, but she's been sticking to me like a shadow, so I told her she could come. I wish now I hadn't.

We went over to the hospital and picked up Mrs. Peterson's car. (She doesn't know I can't drive.) Every two minutes Joy wanted to know where we were going. She hoped I was going to split, I guess. I told her that it would be fun to ride around for a while.

We drove across the bridge and down the shore to the beach shack, about 300 feet beyond where the heroin was buried. I parked the car and told Joy to wait, I had to see an old lady about a white horse.

I hurried back along the road and made as if I were going into the shack. I ducked around it and ran up the beach to the place where I had put the stakes.

It was getting dark but I found them right away. I paced off the distance and began to dig, kicking the sand away first, then using my hands.

The packet was buried deeper than I thought. I felt panicky. What if someone had come along and found it accidentally? I got down on my knees and dug faster, thinking now that I had the wrong place and that in a few minutes it would be too dark to see.

The packet was damp from the day it rained so hard, but as I brushed the sand off I felt sure that water hadn't seeped through.

I was slipping the packet into my blouse when I heard Joy's voice behind me. The next moment she stood not three feet away. I could have reached out and touched her.

Joy has a soft voice. It's slow and soft. "What you doin'?" she asked.

"Nothing," I answered.

It wasn't much of an answer, considering the fact that there was a pile of scraped-up sand at my feet, a big hole, and a package in my hand.

"What you messin' with?" Joy said in her soft voice, the way people talk who come from Texas.

"Something I buried," I said.

"Valuables?" Joy asked.

She must have known what I had in my hand. Sometime she might have seen a packet just like it.

Just a few steps beyond us was a bank that the sea had cut away last week when the tides were heavy and I had worried about them washing the stash away. They had come close.

Joy reached out and put a hand on the package. The surf was breaking so loud I couldn't hear what she said.

I felt like running, but I knew that even though

she was heavy, she would catch me. I remembered the story Jeffrey had told me about the girl who had pretended to throw the gold charm into the snowbank. I thought about it suddenly.

Joy touched my shoulder. "You've got something valuable," she said. She was talking faster now and louder. "Let me see it."

I turned away and raised my hand and made a motion of throwing the package. A wave was running back to the sea, dragging bunches of kelp with it. Joy must have thought it was dragging the package, because she jumped over the bank and ran down the beach, waving her arms and screaming.

I stuffed the heroin under my sweater and walked out to where Joy was running back and forth.

It was almost dark now. Only a faint streak of red showed along the horizon, and some light came from a fishing boat anchored beyond the breakers. It was seining for croakers, and light from a string of lanterns rippled across the water and up the beach.

Joy stopped screaming. She raised her arms toward the sea, then she let them drop at her sides.

I waded out and stood beside her. Streamers of kelp tugged at our legs. Waves came in and went out. Neither one of us said anything for a long while. Then Joy began to mutter over and over, "Why, Hilary? Why did you do that?"

She kept muttering this all the way to the car and while we were driving back to the hospital. She never waited for me to answer. It was just as well she didn't.

December 1

The packet isn't heavy but it's awkward, and I had to carry it around all day under my sweater, which I kept buttoned. Last night I had it in bed with me, and I'll have it again tonight. But I can't keep on this way. Joy or someone is sure to find out.

December 2

This morning on the way to work I stashed the heroin. Just across the street from where I get off the bus, near the entrance to Balboa Park.

I went inside and walked around until I found a tree off by itself with some dead needles underneath. I hid the package among the dead needles and made sure that no one saw me. I've been hanging on to it now for weeks. Why? I don't intend to sell it. I don't intend to use it. Then why do I go to all this trouble and maybe ask for danger? In the back of my mind do I plan to use it someday? Deep down, do I still have the urge? I thought I had lost it back in San Carlos when Sybil offered me a snort and I refused. But did I?

I should talk to Jane Forsythe. I'll tell her the truth. I'm tired of lying.

December 3

A man named Ken Welch, who supervises Tranquillity and the other halfway houses in the county, came by today. It's the first time I've seen him.

He's about the age my father would be. He has a bald head, except for a fringe of hair that hangs over his collar. He smiles a lot and looks at you when he talks, as if you meant something to him. As if you were a real person.

I liked him right away.

I'd lied to Miss Forsythe. When she asked about my parents, I said that they lived in Colorado.

But for some reason I decided not to lie to Mr. Welch. I told him the truth. Everything. Even about Ramón and my baby and my mother. Everything except the heroin. I must have talked for an hour.

"Are you going back home?" he asked me.

"No," I said.

"What about your mother? Have you called her?"

"No."

"You should. Remember, she's your legal guardian. It will make a difference in the way we handle your probation, if you're released in her custody. I can call her, if you want me to, and ask her to come down, but it's better if you see her yourself."

December 4

A new problem. Story in the *Union* this morning about preparations for Christmas. Next week city crews will start to decorate the pine trees at Balboa Park. This means that the cache of heroin is not safe. I'll have to get myself over there and move it somewhere. Either that or just take a chance that the workmen won't find it.

But if they do, what then? Wouldn't it solve a lot of things?

December 7

I went over to the park this afternoon. They were putting lights on the trees. I waited around and picked up the packet without much trouble. The park is not a safe place to hide it again, not with Christmas crowds running around everywhere.

But I can't keep it here in my room. Not much longer, anyway.

Pretty soon Joy and I graduate. If you can call it that.

I'm supposed to leave a few days before Joy does, but Ken Welch has consented to let me stay over. The Family plans a party for us. A feast—hot dogs, ice cream, and a five-layer cake with candles!

In some ways leaving will be sad, but the big thing is I won't be going back to jail. I'll try to find a better job than I have at Taco Kitchen. Maybe I can find a job for Joy somewhere. The last few days she hasn't talked so much about taking off. The problem now is to play it cool. Not foul up.

December 11

I've been thinking about my talk with Mr. Welch and have decided to take his advice.

I'll go out tomorrow to see Mother. Tomorrow is Saturday and she'll be home, probably grading papers. This is better, much as I hate it, than having her come down here and find me in an institution. Not behind bars, but practically.

December 12

Today was supposed to be the day. I worried about it all night.

How was I to explain all that's happened? How and why am I now residing at Tranquillity House? And how I will be residing there for another week or more, providing I'm lucky. And Mother listening with that I-told-you-so look on her face. The runaway daughter returns and is forgiven and all that. Luckily, I couldn't get away.

December 13

Big headline in the paper this morning. A ring's been operating here in San Diego. Extorting money from the parents of runaway girls. The head of it is Albert Herman, owner of Point Loma Sea Foods. Mr. Herman and his son, Teddy, have both been taken into custody.

Kind Mr. Herman, Mother's friend.

December 14

I must call Sybil's mother. But what will I say? Joy follows me around like a puppy. Her mother and father must have had high hopes for her when they named her Joy.

December 15

When Joy came out of the bathroom this morning, she saw me sitting on the edge of the bed staring into space.

She gave me some dopey advice about cheering up, the worst was yet to come. I felt like bashing her one but instead I asked her if she would come along, I was going out to see Mother.

She's gotten awfully friendly lately. I think she'd do anything I asked her to do, like walking through a forest fire with a wildcat under each arm. I didn't let on about the dope I was taking along.

We caught the Point Loma bus, which stops within two blocks of our house, and walked up the hill. It was a hot day in spite of its being December. The house looked just the same, though I felt as if I'd been gone for years.

A cocker spaniel sitting on the porch barked

at us as we came up the walk and kept barking when I rang the bell. I remembered that Mother always wanted a watchdog.

No one answered the bell, so I went around in back. The garage was open but the car was gone. When I came back, Joy was talking to little Linda Sanders from up the block. I hadn't been friendly with Linda, but I was happy to see her, happier I guess than she was to see me, judging from the startled look on her face.

"Where's Mother?" I asked her.

Linda shook her head. She was always shy. Never one to come right out and answer a question until she got started. Then she never stopped.

"Her car's gone," I said.

"She's gone," Linda said.

"Where?"

"I don't know. In the East somewhere. In Chicago, I think."

"Chicago?"

"I had a card from her, like two weeks ago. She said she was going to Chicago and would write me when she got there. I haven't heard since, but I expect to. She's good at writing. I've had two cards from her already. One from Denver and one from Kansas City. She heard you were in Kansas City. The police, someone, saw you there in Kansas City. And you were in Denver, too."

I started to say that I had never been in Denver or Kansas City either. "Did Mother leave the key?"

Linda looked blank. "What key?"

"The key to the house. Did she leave it with your mother?"

"She sold the house," Linda said. "It belongs to Mr. Montgomery. He's Navy. They just moved in. They're from San Francisco. They haven't any children. Only the dog. His name is Pearl."

Pearl was still barking as Joy and I walked away.

December 16

I didn't feel like writing any more last night when we got back, so I'll finish now.

We left Linda and the barking dog that belonged to some people named Montgomery and walked down to the bus stop. It was still hot, but a sweet-smelling breeze was blowing in from the sea.

I stood there looking at our house up on the hill—at the house that had been ours once and now belonged to someone else. I thought about Mother. I thought about the night in the Gatito Café when I had run when she called my name. About the notices in the newspaper that begged me to come home. About her giving up her teaching job and then traveling around the country, following rumors. . . .

I thought of all these things. I thought of them

all at once, not one after another. And I didn't really think of them. They weren't thoughts, really. They were just something inside me, lying there in a big lump.

The bus showed up finally, but we didn't get on. Joy and I walked down to the wharf. We passed Mr. Herman's fish shop. It was closed and had a sign on the door. I didn't bother to read it.

There were some boats tied up at the wharf unloading fish. I walked past them to a place where there weren't any boats and took the packet of heroin out of my sweater and gave it to Joy and told her what it was and how I had fooled her on the beach.

She turned pale. "What do you want me to do?"

"Throw it away," I said.

Joy looked at the roll of heroin in her hand. Then she looked at me. She acted as if I had asked her to throw herself in the water.

"Where?"

"In the bay."

Joy held on to the packet. She ran her finger over the waxy paper, talking to herself. It wouldn't have surprised me any to see her turn and run.

"Throw it," I said.

"You," she said, holding the packet out to me.

"Throw it as far as you can." Now I was shouting.

Joy raised her arm. She looked at me for a

moment, as if she expected me to change my mind. I waited. I wondered if she had the strength. I wondered if I had the strength.

Then she moaned and sent the packet spinning, far out into the bay.

There were three sea gulls hovering over us, and they swooped down as the packet struck the water. They must have thought it was a fish. Anyway, one of them got the thing in its beak. The two other gulls flew down and the three of them fought and shrieked over it until nothing was left but shreds of paper.

I stood there on the wharf and watched the paper floating on the water. Joy stood beside me. I hadn't thought of the *Ancient Mariner* for a long time. I don't know why I thought about it now.

I said the words out loud. Almost the last words of the poem:

"He prayeth best, who loveth best
All things both great and small;
For the dear God who loveth us,
He made and loveth all."

Joy must have thought I had gone crazy. Crazy, crazy. But she didn't say anything. She just held on to my hand. We both held on and walked away from the bay and the wharf and the screaming gulls.